A SENTIMENTAL NOTION

A SENTIMENTAL NOTION

•

JAN McDANIEL

AVALON BOOKS
THOMAS BOUREGY AND COMPANY, INC.
401 LAFAYETTE STREET
NEW YORK, NEW YORK 10003

PRINTED IN THE UNITED STATES OF AMERICA
ON ACID-FREE PAPER
BY HADDON CRAFTSMEN, SCRANTON, PENNSYLVANIA

To Linda Baker and Jeff Riddle,
who are among the best of friends.

Chapter One

Puzzling over how to put her life back together, Dale Addison was too preoccupied to sense one more disaster coming.

Absently, she shifted Gerard's leash from one hand to the other to accommodate the sliding sheaf of manila envelopes tucked under her arm. The St. Bernard's attention, however, was riveted on a squirrel up ahead.

Dale continued up the sidewalk, hoping this batch of resumes was going to pay off. Her grandparents had been kind to allow her to stay with them these past few months. But she couldn't intrude forever, and her small savings account was nearly depleted.

Just less than six months ago, she'd had everything going for her. A good job with what she had believed was a future, her own apartment, a close-knit circle of friends.

She hadn't done anything wrong, yet her life had skidded to a standstill. No job. No apartment. Her friends miles away.

A sharp tug on Gerard's leash jerked her back to the present and nearly off her feet.

"Hey, Gerard!" she complained, looking down to find him straining to get at the squirrel.

In response, he pulled harder.

Seeing he was not going to be cajoled into obedience, she took a firmer tone. "No, Gerard. . . ." When that didn't work, she added, "Please!"

Her grandfather had suggested she bring the dog along to the mailbox.

Now Gerard pulled harder, leaving her no choice but to release the letters so she could grasp the leash with both hands. Her neatly addressed envelopes fluttered to the sidewalk.

The heels of her running shoes planted solidly on the ground, she fought to restrain the huge canine.

But she was no match for him.

He pulled harder, and she skid into a not-so-graceful sitting position on the easement.

Stunned, she gradually realized the leash's handle was no longer in her hand. Panic overcame her. Gramps would be devastated if she returned home without his cherished pet.

Fortunately, Gerard was standing beside her. Marveling at the novelty of having her at eye-level, he had forgotten the squirrel.

Not seeing the leash nearby, Dale slowly rose to one knee, crooning Gerard's name before she lunged at him and made a flying tackle.

Undaunted by his capture, Gerard turned and gave her a slurpy dog kiss across the face.

"Quit it!" she protested, pushing back the slobbering dog and groping for the leash.

He was as big as a bear. She would never understand why her grandfather insisted on owning such a monster.

It occurred to her how comical she must look wrestling this beast.

Well, at least there were no witnesses.

But the sound of footsteps on the pavement evaporated that hope. "Are you all right?" an unfamiliar male voice inquired.

Dale's cheeks burned. Better if she could just get up and unobtrusively slink away.

"Terrific," she answered, too embarrassed to look up. "Thanks."

Before she could object, he had stooped over and was gathering her envelopes. *Great.* Not only had this stranger glimpsed her clumsiness, now he would know she was applying for work with every major company in North America.

"I can get those," she said feebly.

"No problem," he replied, without stopping.

His eyes swung toward her, and Dale felt a jolt as her glance collided with a sharp-featured face softened by eyes the color of hot cocoa. She liked the face—serious yet appealing.

Then she realized she was still kneeling on the ground, hugging the dog.

Quickly, she released Gerard's neck, coiling the end of his leash around her wrist.

A hand reached down to her.

"Here," the man offered.

Because he was so willing to help, she believed that—although she was fully capable of rising under her own power—she would insult him if she refused his assistance.

Hesitantly, she placed a slender hand in his larger one. His grip was firm. He cradled her elbow in his other hand as he hoisted her to her feet.

Dale's heart sped up. Silly, she thought. She had never reacted this way to someone she didn't know. She told herself she was simply reacting to his kindness, not to him.

She smiled. "Thank you," she said, brushing grass off her clothing.

Gerard began sniffing the stranger's shoe.

Dale gasped. "Stop it, Gerard," she commanded, yanking his chain.

Gerard ignored her.

The stranger laughed. "Gerard must have cut his classes at obedience school," he noted.

He had an easy, genuine smile.

"He's not my dog, or believe me, I'd trade him in," Dale assured him. Gerard stared up at her sweetly. "He's still a puppy," she added gently. Even though the dog was impossible, she had developed a fondness for him.

"Listen, are you sure you're all right? You took quite a spill."

So, he must have seen it all.

Although she felt a bit sore, she wasn't about to admit it.

"I'm all right," she replied.

"You're bleeding."

She followed his glance to her shorts-clad leg. Her knee and calf were scraped.

"That's nothing. I'll tend to it when I get home."

"I'm parked just around the corner if you need a ride."

"No, thanks. I live down the block, and I'm really not hurt. It was my own fault, anyway." She shrugged. "I wasn't paying enough attention to Gerard. By the time I tried to stop him, it was too late."

Brown eyes danced as the man shook his head. "And after you said please and everything."

Dale colored, her skin matching her orange tank top. "I didn't think anyone was listening."

Now it was his turn to shift uneasily.

He handed her the envelopes. "Sorry. Here. These don't seem to be damaged."

"Thanks," she said, accepting the stack with renewed embarrassment. Was he going to comment on these too?

Fortunately, he didn't.

Disturbed with the lack of attention he was getting, Gerard suddenly decided to make friends with the stranger too. Without warning, he sprung up on two legs, propping dirty paws on the man's three-piece suit.

Dale's eyes widened in horror.

"Down, Gerard," she ordered so harshly the dog obeyed instantly.

"I'm sorry," she apologized, eyeing the dirty paw prints on the man's jacket. Her impulse was to brush at them, but she thought better of it. "I'll have the suit cleaned for you."

He waved her off. "There's no need. Really."

He inched away from both her and the dog.

"Are you sure?"

"It was about ready to go to the cleaners anyway." He continued backing away.

"Well, thank you for helping," Dale called.

"As long as you're not hurt," he said.

Dale watched him walk off, wondering what a man in business attire was doing in a residential neighborhood at midday. Probably a bill-collector or insurance salesman.

Attractive though. Unusually so.

Her heart was still beating a little faster than normal.

Was it any wonder? Her life was so abysmally dull, this was the most interesting thing that had happened to her all day. All week in fact.

She tucked the envelopes back under her arm and issued Gerard an edict to behave. "See what you've done?" she scolded the dog.

She sighed heavily as she continued on her way. She was becoming envious of people who had an office to go to each morning. She missed having her own apartment, living in the city and visiting friends. She missed working, feeling she was accomplishing something with her life.

With a sigh, she approached the mailbox, watching her letters slide down the chute like chunks of snow in an avalanche. All she knew was she couldn't sit back and feel like a victim, dwelling on her loss. To get by until a good position came through, she was going to have to take the first job she could find. Whatever it was.

"I don't know why they have to hold this meeting at night instead of in the afternoon," Dale's grandfather complained from the passenger seat beside her. "Probably hoping I won't go, so Mace Travers can pull one over on me. They all know I hate driving at night."

Dale steered her dark blue Grand Am through a left turn and sighed. Gramps would never admit he couldn't see in the dark any more. "I don't mind driving you, Gramps. Who is Mace Travers, and why wouldn't he want you at the meeting?"

"He's an outsider who doesn't give an owl's hoot about Meadowside and managed to get himself elected to the town council last year."

Dale laughed softly. Her window was partially down, and a cool, late-August breeze brushed her face. Orange streaked the sky as the sun began to set. "He must care about something if people voted for him. And doesn't he have to live here to be elected?"

Her grandfather shook his head. "Well, he hasn't lived here long. A couple years is all. Opened up a plant outside town, making fancy lamps and chandeliers. Nobody would run against him is how he won. This town has taken a sad turn since the old days. Nobody takes pride in their hometown any more."

"Sounds like Mr. Travers is trying to."

"Hmmph. Trying to ruin the place is all. To him, everything has to be new and improved. He has no respect for tradition."

"Gramps, the world has opened up. People have a

larger sense of the world. Maybe you should meet him halfway.''

Sam Guthrie snorted. ''Seems like a lot of room to flounder in. When I was growing up, people had everything they needed in one spot—friends, stores, entertainment. People needed each other. They didn't lock themselves up at night and stare at television sets.''

Dale sighed. She wasn't in the mood to argue the pros and cons of television with Gramps. Besides, there was no winning against him. Even the most brilliant argument wouldn't sway him once he'd made his mind up about something.

''So what do you think this Mace Travers wants to put over on you?'' she asked.

''He wants to whittle the fall festival, Meadowside's biggest event of the year, to one day instead of a weekend like it's always been.''

Dale's expression brightened. ''I remember coming here to that festival one year, Mom and Dad and I. I was awfully small, but I remember riding the carousel.''

Gramps' tone softened. ''One of the best years of the fair. You were about five years old. I remember you had your hair tied back in pigtails with ribbons and they streamed out behind you when you rode that carousel. You held your head up real high, pretending it was a real horse. You cried when your mom said it was time to go home.''

"Did I really?"

He nodded. "Even back then, you had a mind of your own. Big dreams. You said you were going to go out west and own a ranch someday, just like Dale Evans, the actress you were named after."

Dale laughed. "Thank goodness we don't have to stick with the choices we make in kindergarten. If I remember correctly, I was also fascinated with dinosaurs." But a wave of sadness rippled through her. Where had all her big dreams taken her? To a corporate layoff and long-term unemployment?

"Don't worry, Dale," her grandfather consoled her. "In time, the right job will come along."

Dale shook her head. As hard-headed as her grandfather could be, sometimes he had the oddest knack of being able to read her mind.

"I thought I might look for something around here until a real job comes through."

"Not much around here besides waitressing or cashiering. Not exactly what you went to college for."

She chewed her lip. "I'm starting to wonder what I did go to college for."

Her grandfather gave her a hard look. "It doesn't take much of a person to hold up in good times. Keeping your dignity in hard times requires grit."

"Oh, I know. I could be worse off. You and Grandma have been so good to me. But I'm twenty-six years old. I've got to move on with my life."

"We enjoy having you stay with us. For as long as it takes, understand?"

"Yes." She managed a grateful smile.

"It's almost like when Linda was here."

"But I'm not Mom," she reminded him quickly. She felt guilty about remembering so little of her mother, who died when Dale was six. Her father had raised her alone, with minimal help from a part-time housekeeper. They had been close. Then, without warning, while Dale was away at college, her dad had gotten remarried and moved to Oregon.

Dale had met her stepmother a few times, and liked her well enough. But the close relationship between her and her father had been severed. His failure to share his plans had broken the trust between them. Dale couldn't help feeling as though he had been waiting anxiously for her to leave so he could get on with his life. And his absence left a void in hers.

Which was why when the concert promoter she had worked for cut back half its staff, including her, and she could no longer afford her one-bedroom apartment, she had gladly accepted her grandparents' invitation. She had nowhere else to go.

"Anyone can see that. You look like her, but you're more outgoing and independent. You take after your dad that way."

"Were you upset with Dad when he married Mom and moved her to New York?"

Gramps fell silent for a moment, shaking his head. "At the time, your grandmother and I thought Linda was too young to get married. Knowing now she had only a little time left, we're glad she lived it as she wanted to."

"No one ever knows what's in store for them, I guess."

"Losing a child is life's hardest ordeal. I know you'd probably rather not have to be here, but to your grandmother and I your stay is like a gift of fate. We haven't seen enough of you over the years."

Dale smiled, blinking back tears. She'd never heard Gramps get so sentimental. He must be mellowing in his old age.

She eased the car into the parking lot beside city hall. Several others were already there.

"I can come back and pick you up," she offered.

"No sense driving all the way home. The meeting shouldn't last long. Besides, we'll be going over plans for the festival. Come on in, maybe you can offer some suggestions."

Dale considered. Her current batch of resumes mailed, she certainly didn't have anything pressing to do. And considering her financial situation, shopping was out of the question.

"All right," she agreed.

Ten minutes later, she sat among a handful of spectators seated in the city's meeting room when the door opened and in walked the stranger who had helped her out that afternoon.

He had changed suits, she noticed, guiltily remembering Gerard's earlier shenanigans.

Immediately he spotted her. Smiling, he approached her chair.

As he neared, warmth rippled through her as it had this afternoon. He certainly had an aura about him. She admired the way he carried himself, straight but not stiff.

"So we meet again, Ms. Addison," he greeted her.

Dale's expression went blank. How did he know her name?

"I read one of your address labels," he confessed. "Your name just kind of jumped out at me."

"It was good of you to help me this afternoon."

"What brings you to the council meeting?"

"Actually, I brought my grandfather. He's on the council, Sam Guthrie." She nodded in her grandfather's direction.

His smile faded. "You're Sam's granddaughter?" He sounded incredulous.

Dale couldn't understand his shock.

"Yes, I am."

At this point, she was hoping he might identify himself.

But she was disappointed. For the first time, he struggled for words. "Well, I'm glad Sam found a ride. He declined my offer to pick him up. It's good to see you again," he finished, quickly turning away.

Dale realized he was once again walking off without telling her his name.

But she wasn't left wondering for long. He rounded the head table and took his seat behind the nameplate "Mason Travers."

Chapter Two

Mace busied himself taking papers out of his briefcase and shuffling them, hiding behind the open lid.

Sam's granddaughter? He couldn't believe it!

The young woman seated a few feet away had caught his attention more than anyone had in a long time. This afternoon he'd stifled his amusement long enough to admire her spunk as she wrestled that goofy canine. And despite the dog's antics, she'd maintained her dignity the best she could.

Something about her had intrigued him, and it went beyond hair the color of maple syrup spilling over her shoulders, sea blue eyes sparkling behind a fringe of long, dark lashes, the upturned nose accenting a small mouth. Even though she had traded in her shorts, T-shirt and scuffed running shoes for a plaid dress this evening, he had recognized her immediately. In fact, he had been remembering her off and on all afternoon, despite his efforts to push her out of his mind.

Finding her here had been his great luck, he'd thought.

But it was no great luck that she was Sam's granddaughter. Sam, the most cantankerous old-timer Mace had ever encountered, had opposed every suggestion Mace made since he was sworn in. And Mace knew Sam was going to be especially upset with what he was about to propose tonight. Would Sam's granddaughter side with the old man and call off their friendship before it began? he wondered.

Well, business first. He couldn't let that possibility prevent him from serving the town's best interest. And in the long run, his curiosity about Ms. Addison was best left untapped.

Staving off his cowardice, he shut his briefcase. Dale flashed him a smile.

He smiled back. Apparently she wasn't aware he and her grandfather were rivals. Well, she soon would.

Her smile dropped abruptly.

Puzzled, Mace followed her eyes in Sam's direction.

Sam was scowling at her. He swung his glare sideways to Mace.

Mace dropped his eyes and shuffled papers again. *If Sam had his way, citizens of Meadowside would still be riding in carriages, pumping well water, and read-ing by candlelight,* Mace thought.

To Mace's relief, the chairman called the meeting to order.

Through the routine business, he couldn't help glancing at Dale. She was more appealing than the two reporters who lined the front row with their cameras and tape recorders.

"The next thing on our agenda," Zelda Smithers, the chairman, announced, "is the fall festival."

Here it comes, Mace thought, bracing himself. "I suggest the secretary read the report on last year's fes-tival," he said quickly.

"All right," Zelda agreed, directing the town sec-retary to read the report. By the time she finished, Mace's point was clear. Because of low attendance, the town treasury had barely broken even.

"If it gets any worse, we'll be dipping into tax rev-enues to fund a festival nobody's interested in," Mace summarized. "I say let's skip the festival this year."

Sam was on his feet immediately. "In the seventy-two years I've lived in this town, we've always had a fall festival. Used to be good ones until the city started skimping on everything."

Mace turned to him. "It's not working any more, Sam," he insisted, avoiding letting his eyes stray into the audience.

Sam grew livid. "People don't go any more because

you bring in those idiotic carnival rides and games. There's nothing for anyone over thirteen. I say, let's do it and do it right.'' He pounded his fist on the table for emphasis.

Dale cringed. *A little overkill, Gramps,* she thought.

Mace noticed her discomfort. Of course, he thought, she would be intelligent and objective enough to see his point rather than automatically siding with her grandfather.

Zelda pounded her gavel. ''Let's not turn this into another squabble,'' she suggested. ''You've each made a good point. We can't continue funding a money-losing venture, Sam. But Mace, people here expect a festival. Sam's not the only person who will be disappointed if we don't have one.''

Sidney Snowden, a lanky white-haired man who so far had been sitting quietly with his head propped on one arm, spoke up. ''Sounds like we need to have a festival and ensure it's a money-maker. Talk about being between a rock and a hard place.''

Mace smiled faintly. ''Show me the person who can pull that off and I'll hire him to run my company.''

Dale didn't see the problem as being that comical. Proper planning was all that was required.

''Maybe you should. Seems you were in charge of last year's festival, Mace,'' Sam piped up. ''And all you did was bring in the carnival.''

Mace colored. At the time, he'd been swamped at

the plant, working nearly round the clock and running on a few hours sleep each night. Believing the festival was not that important, he hadn't devoted much attention to it.

"I admit, I took the folder from the year before and just followed that plan. I think if you'll look back, you'll admit it hasn't been much of an event for several years."

Calvin Shepherd, seated on the end beside Mace, scratched his chin. "Maybe it's time to let it die quietly. None of us really has time to work with it."

"Confound it, Calvin," Sam protested. "Pretty soon we'll be a bunch of strangers just living in the same town together. The festival's one time a year people get out and meet their neighbors. Meadowside's starting to feel more like a big city every day."

"Obviously if we do it at all, we need to devote some thought and resources to it. I'm not sure, Sam, whether any of us is up to tackling a job like that," Zelda considered.

Dale, unable to sit back any longer, was suddenly on her feet. She stepped up to the microphone.

"Excuse me," she said, unsure how she was supposed to address the council. "My name is Dale Addison. I'm just living here temporarily, but it seems to me all of you want this town to be a better place. Other business people do too, so why don't you ask them to pitch in and help sponsor the festival?"

Zelda raised a brow and nodded. "That's worth considering."

Dale, comfortable in her own area of expertise, continued enthusiastically. "The reason you're not making any money on the festival is you're providing a carnival, something people can go to just about any day of the year if they really want to. What draws crowds is something unique. People today want something they can't get anywhere else. Celebrity appearances are always popular."

Calvin chuckled. "What celebrity is going to come here, the weatherman from the television news?"

Sam spoke up. "Well, Dale here knows all those famous recording stars and what have you. She's spent the past three years working with them."

Dale paled as she felt eyes turning to her with new interest. She took a step back.

"Is that true, Ms. Addison?" Mace asked.

Dale stepped forward again. "Yes. But I wasn't volunteering to book anybody for you. Most entertainers schedule appearances far in advance of the few weeks we're talking about. And they charge a big fee."

"Besides," countered Calvin. "Who's going to pull everything together and go around trying to convince our merchants to participate? I was chairman year before last, and I don't have the time to do it again."

"Nobody wants you to," Sam quipped.

Chaos broke loose, with everybody talking at once. Zelda banged the gavel again. "Come on," she coaxed. "This isn't getting us anywhere. Why not take the money budgeted for the festival expenses and hire a consultant to run it? If we make money, we'll continue holding a festival. If we don't, we'll scrap it next year. Fair enough?"

Silence fell over the room.

"It sounds reasonable to me," Mace agreed finally. "Sam?"

"Yeah," Sam grumbled.

Zelda made a motion to that effect. Mace seconded it, and the group passed it unanimously. At least they were all agreeing on something, Dale noted.

"Any suggestions on who we can hire?" Zelda asked, jotting notes on a yellow legal pad.

Mace's eyes swooped down on Dale, who had returned to her seat during the voting.

"I don't think there's any question," he decreed, "but that we should employ Sam's granddaughter."

To Dale's astonishment, it was her grandfather who zapped that suggestion. "No," he protested. "We can't do that."

"I hope you understand," Gramps apologized on the way home.

"Sure. I do. Completely," Dale assured him.

Within seconds she'd gotten a job only to have it slip out of her grasp with equal speed.

"If you were anybody but my granddaughter, I would have voted to hire you in a second," he explained. "But the voters would wonder why I was using my seat on the council to employ relatives. It wouldn't be right."

Dale agreed.

But because she knew she could save the festival for her grandfather and she wanted to do this for him, she had consented to oversee the event as a volunteer. Still as unemployed as ever, she had a big job ahead of her.

Mace had shaken her hand before he left, coolly congratulating her on her new appointment. His brusqueness puzzled her. Hadn't he suggested her for the job to begin with?

She guided the car into the ribbon drive of her grandparents' two-story brick bungalow. She liked their shady street with its older homes bordered by lilac bushes and evergreens, the broad front porches and fenced yards. People certainly had more room here than they did in New York. And the air was fresh and clean.

The outside light, equipped with a motion detector, went on as she pulled up by the side door.

"Why didn't you tell me Mace Travers offered you a ride this evening?" she asked her grandfather as she unbuckled her seat belt.

Gramps eyed her warily. "Didn't think it was worth mentioning," he replied.

"Maybe you should give him a chance. I don't think he's out to destroy the town. After all, he was the one who suggested I take charge of the festival."

"It was a trick. He was trying to discredit me with the voters by getting me to vote to hire you."

"I don't think the conflict of interest occurred to him. He was just trying to give the festival a fair chance to survive."

Gramps grunted. "Or maybe he thinks you can't possibly carry it off and he can end it for good."

Dale looked over at her grandfather. "I don't believe that. He seemed sincere enough to me."

"That's how he's devious. He comes off as charming and is as dangerous as mislabeled arsenic. You steer clear of him, young lady. He never lets anything stop him from accomplishing what he wants."

Dale smiled. "You just described ninety percent of the people in New York, Gramps. There's nothing wrong with ambition."

"Well, this is Meadowside, not New York. Life moves a little slower here. There's a difference between being ambitious and trampling on other people's lives."

"That doesn't make him the devil." Dale wondered what Mace had done to inspire Sam's bitterness toward him.

"What's he doing here then, if he thinks we're so backward? What's he hiding from?"

"He probably just thought this was a good place for a factory," she concluded.

The night air was pleasantly cool against her bare arms. She sniffed a hint of autumn. The rural Indiana countryside would probably look spectacular in its autumn foliage. Already she'd noticed some leaves turning russet. Too bad she probably wouldn't be here to see the transformation. Couldn't be here to see it.

Surely, she would get a job before then.

She had explained to the council that she might have to leave before the festival was held the first weekend in October.

As she opened the side door, Gerard came bounding out to greet them.

"Down, boy," she commanded, patting the dog on the head.

Over the slices of chocolate-marshmallow cake and glasses of milk her grandmother had waiting for them, she and Sam filled Rachel in on Dale's new duties.

"I'm so excited," Rachel noted. "Your grandfather and I met at that festival. I was visiting friends here that weekend and he stepped up and asked me to dance as soon as the band struck up Friday night. We stayed together through the rest of the festival, and when the booths were being taken down, he proposed."

Dale's face lit up. She looked at her grandfather with amazement.

"So quickly?" she asked. "How absolutely romantic." She wondered if her grandmother was describing the same man who a few moments ago had complained about life moving too fast.

"Nah," countered Gramps. "It was wartime. I was about to go overseas. Never knew who'd be coming back. You didn't dawdle around. If you were in love you had to know it. Never had any regrets either."

"It sounds like one of those old movies. I didn't know things like that used to happen in real life," Dale told them. No wonder the festival meant so much to him. Gramps was more sentimental than she had ever given him credit for. She used to think he was just a grouchy old man.

"Oh, Sam," his wife protested, shaking her head. "It was romantic," she told Dale. "He swept me off my feet. And I'm sure the same thing happens to young people today."

Dale found it hard to imagine her grandfather making grand gestures to anyone. But wouldn't it be her grandmother who had triggered that side of him? If anyone looked at the world through the proverbial rose-colored glasses, she did.

Rachel surrounded herself with lace curtains, linen table clothes and embroidered pillowcases. She collected figures of elves and clowns and animals, constructing an imaginative miniature universe in curio cabinets throughout the house. Of course she believed in things like love at first sight and true love. And for her, it had worked.

While Dale envied her grandmother's simpler view of life, she knew it didn't work for her. Dreams didn't just fall into place like in the storybooks. Disappointments crept into your life, and only plain old work could keep you going. There was no magic remedy.

Dale drained the last of her milk.

"More cake?" Rachel offered.

"No, thank you," Dale answered, thinking she probably shouldn't have indulged in the first piece. Her grandmother's baking was nearly impossible to resist. "I've got a phone call to make."

She said goodnight to her grandparents and went upstairs to use the phone where it was quiet. The third bedroom had been converted into a study, one corner piled with Sam's model railroad magazines.

The bedroom she slept in had once been her mother's room. Dale had tried to imagine her mother as a girl, sleeping there. But the vision eluded her.

She checked her watch and wrote down the time so she would be able to reimburse her grandparents for the long distance call.

To her astonishment, the phone rang just as she was poised to lift the receiver.

"Hello?" she said.

"Dale Addison, please."

She knew it was Mace's voice. The delight she felt at hearing it surprised her. "This is Dale."

He identified himself, then apologized for calling so late. "I realized I had some open time on my schedule tomorrow morning, and I thought it might help you if I show you the park where the festival is held."

"That's generous of you," she agreed. "I'll accept as much help as I can get. What time?"

"Around ten?"

"Fine. And listen, I want you to know I had no problem with the matter of hiring you. This is a load of work to do for free. I think everything would have been fine as long as Sam abstained from voting."

"Well, thanks. I need something to do anyway, and the festival means a lot to my grandparents. I really don't mind."

"I'll see you tomorrow then."

A thread of excitement spun through her at the prospect of seeing him. His charm was indeed working on her. Still, she remembered her grandfather's warning. Why would Sam think this man was dangerous?

"Yes, thanks."

She replaced the receiver.

She liked Mace's voice, his face, his walk, his seeming sense of fair play. But she knew she was in no position to get too attached to anyone right now.

Putting her life back in order had to remain her first priority.

Cutting short her daydream about Mace, she opened her address book to a familiar number. She really didn't relish making this call. A boat sailed best if it wasn't rocked.

Then she thought of how pleased Gramps would be if she ensured the longevity of his beloved fall festival.

Resolutely, she picked up the phone. It was four hours earlier in California, but she doubted Johnny would be home. To her surprise, he answered on the second ring.

"Johnny?" she asked.

"Dale?" he asked. "Where in Jupiter are you? I called the agency a few weeks ago and Maria said you'd left."

"Layoffs—by seniority. I'm unemployed and staying in Indiana."

"That would make a good song title—'Unemployed in Indiana.' You might as well be on Jupiter."

"It's not so bad here, really. I'm here with my grandparents."

"This is Dale Addison, isn't it?"

She laughed.

"You're not playing bingo and square dancing, are you?"

"Not yet."

"Actually, I'm envious. I wish my grandparents were still alive so I could visit them."

"Listen, Johnny, I need a favor."

"This is a red-letter day. You've never asked for anything before. Name it, Cowgirl."

The old nickname evoked a smile. Dale had once made the mistake of revealing her namesake to him and had been dubbed Cowgirl thereafter.

"You shouldn't agree too quickly. I need you to come to Indiana."

"Wow. That is a big one."

"I know. But I really need you here." And she proceeded to tell him the story she had heard tonight for the first time, about two people who met one night at the harvest festival and fell in love forever.

Chapter Three

Mace arrived at her grandparents' doorstep promptly at ten. He was dressed casually in jeans, leather hiking boots, and a green cotton shirt.

His appearance pleased Dale, who had decided her own jeans, tennis shoes, and chambray shirt topped by a suede newsboy cap were suitable for traipsing around in the park.

"Hi," he greeted her cheerfully as she opened the door. His eyes swept over her, and Dale felt her stomach fluttering absurdly. He looked every inch as handsome now as he had in his business attire. Streaks of morning sunlight played through his wheat-colored hair.

"Hi," she returned. "Come on in."

He stepped inside reluctantly, as though expecting someone to jump out at him. He smelled of soap and spice.

Dale felt her heart lurch. What was wrong with her?

An apron-clad Rachel appeared from out of the kitchen. "Good morning, Mace. Would you like some coffee? I have some fresh-baked-sweet rolls."

"They are good," Dale assured him.

He held a palm in the air. "No, thanks, really, Mrs. Guthrie. I've already had breakfast and more coffee than I need."

He eyed the entrance to the kitchen warily.

Suddenly, Dale realized he wasn't coming any farther into the house because he guessed Sam was in there. And Mace knew Sam didn't like him. Rachel seemed to like him well enough though, but then Dale had never heard Rachel admit to disliking anyone.

Sam stepped around the corner silently, like a storm cloud slipping into the sky. His expression turned sour the moment he set eyes on Mace.

"Good morning, Mace," he said. "What brings you here?"

Dale laughed, trying to lighten the tension. "I told you Gramps, we're going out to inspect the festival site."

Gramps looked from Dale to Mace, then back again.

"I know that park better than anybody," he insisted. "Maybe I should go with you."

Dale's mouth dropped open. She realized she had been looking forward to having a chance to speak to Mace alone, to unravel some of the mystery Sam had wrapped around him. If nothing else, she was determined to somehow soothe the rift between them. And she wasn't about to endure Sam glowering at Mace all morning.

But she didn't know how to dissuade her grandfather from going. Once he set his mind on something, he wasn't easily diverted.

Fortunately, her grandmother accomplished that for her. ''You're getting a haircut this morning, Sam, remember? I'm sure Dale and Mason can manage on their own.''

''I'll get my portfolio.'' Dale excused herself.

This friction between two grown men was wearing. *Let them stand in the foyer alone for a few minutes and work at treating each other civilly,* she thought.

And what had prompted Gramps to invite himself?

Then she realized her grandfather was mistakenly attempting to protect her from Mace. The uncanny way he had of tuning in to her—of course he sensed she was attracted to Mace. And maybe he was remembering another man long ago who had taken away his only daughter. He could easily assume the same thing was happening to his granddaughter. Well, she couldn't control her reaction to Mace. He was a handsome man with an appealing personality. But she had no intention of running off with him or anyone else. All she wanted was to be on her own again, and only a job offer would lure her away from here.

Surely Gramps wasn't entertaining any illusions about her staying.

Quickly, she retrieved the portfolio from the desk in her room. She had been up late last night, excitement over the festival generating tons of ideas she had hastily scrawled in a notebook.

"I'm ready," she announced brightly as she returned downstairs to find the two men glaring at each other as if ready to do battle. Rachel had wisely and discreetly retreated to the kitchen.

"Have a pleasant day, Sam," Mace told her grandfather.

Sam grunted.

Mace's gold Corvette convertible was parked in the driveway.

"Impressive," Dale told him.

Mace opened the passenger door for her. "I'm really not a showoff. I saw it in the showroom and couldn't talk myself out of it. Actually, I'm a little embarrassed about it. This is the car I would have owned in high school if I could have afforded it. And it's just one more thing your grandfather despises about me," he explained. "You may have noticed I'm not exactly on his list of favorite people."

Dale waited until he was in the car. "So what's with you two anyway?" she asked.

Mace shrugged as the engine purred. "When I moved to town a few years ago, I purchased the land for my factory from the city," he told her, backing the car out of the drive. "The council had to approve the sale. It was a good deal all around. The city wasn't using the property, and I got a good price on it. Sam based his approval on my giving jobs to local people, which I did. I also moved in some skilled craftsmen. I guess Sam had assumed I was hiring locals exclusively and felt betrayed when I didn't. He argued that I could have trained Meadowside residents for those jobs. The kind of training we're talking about takes years, Dale. I was heavily in debt and had to get production into full swing or lose everything I had invested. Sam claims I compromised his principles and undermined the local economy."

"He cares a lot about this town. He's lived here all his life."

"I care about it too. I may have come here from Indianapolis, but I intend to stay."

Dale nodded. "What made you want to locate your business in Meadowside?"

"You know the myths about small-town life. Fresh air, peace and quiet, peace of mind, a sense of community. I thought it would be a better place to live, not only for me, but for my workers as well."

"It probably is if the monotony doesn't drive you bonkers. Personally, I miss Manhattan."

"You can have it. This place has a certain charm. I'm not sorry I moved here. If you're bored, it's because you haven't gotten involved in the community. And we're about to remedy that, aren't we?"

He turned the car down a street lined with large, older homes on sprawling tree-studded lots. Wind streamed through her hair, and the air smelled sweet. It was a gorgeous, golden day.

"Do you want the top up?" he asked.

She tilted her head back to catch the breeze. "No way. I like this."

They drove the rest of the way to the park in silence. The wooded refuge skirting the city limits boasted a fountain, wooden benches, and well-tended flower beds bursting with late-summer blooms.

"How quaint!" she exclaimed, stepping out of the car.

"It's modest, but the city crews take good care of it."

"I wasn't being patronizing. I do like it," she told him.

Mace cleared his throat. He wasn't sure what to think of Dale Addison. She possessed an obvious polish and, like her grandfather, wasn't afraid to speak her mind. Yet she maintained a deep loyalty and affection for those close to her, even to the extent of walking a gigantic dog and working for free.

Reluctantly, he shifted his attention from her to the purpose of their visit. "From what I understand," he said, gesturing to the far end of the park, "in the past, they've placed booths on both sides of this path that circles the park."

Dale nodded, extracting a notebook from the portfolio she had slung over her shoulder by a strap and writing down his suggestion. "Sounds like a good way to keep the crowds moving. I'll have to come back and measure spaces," she said.

"We can walk the path to get an idea of how much room you have," he suggested. "If you want to."

"All right."

She moved toward the tree-lined stone pathway. Mace followed.

Just a few steps down the pathway, and the center of the park seemed far behind. All she heard were birds chirping and Mace's footsteps behind her. The solitude cloaked her with a wonderful sense of tranquility. Reflecting that it was a cliche, she felt close to nature here. For the first time in months, she wasn't fretting over her work situation. Suddenly, she believed everything would work out.

"I didn't even know this park was here," she told Mace, who had caught up to her. "It's the perfect place for the festival. Of course, we'll have to bring in pumpkins and hay and all that. Do you know anyone who has a buggy?

"Excuse me?"

"Carriage rides through the park. Can't you just see people riding through here?"

He was looking at her oddly.

"What's wrong?"

"Nothing. You just didn't strike me before as being a hopeless romantic."

His assessment shocked her. "Me? Never. I'm a realist. But I also know about packaging and selling people what they want. You know, people don't want things or experiences just for the sake of having them necessarily. They want them for the way they expect ownership to make them feel. Your car, for example. You say it embarrasses you, but you wanted it so you could feel seventeen again."

He was standing close, facing her. Dale felt her heart leap disturbingly.

"Touché. Obviously, you're very good at what you do."

"Thank you," she said hesitantly, wondering if she had opened herself too much to him. Now he probably thought she was the most calculating person he'd ever encountered. But that wasn't true. She had learned her marketing job well. "Now if I could just sell some company on my abilities, I'd be all set."

"To be perfectly honest, I don't understand why you're hanging around Meadowside without a job. What happened?"

His eyes were probing hers, and Dale felt a tightness in her throat, a lightness in her head, and a threadiness in her pulse. Who was this man that his proximity affected her very bloodstream?

She had the weirdest impulse to reach up and touch his face. Instead, she backed away and perched on a bench.

To her chagrin, just as she began recovering her senses, he followed and sat down close beside her.

"Is it a secret?" he prodded, attributing her sudden discomfort to his question. "I didn't mean to get too personal."

Dale assumed his nonchalance indicated he hadn't felt anything unusual while standing so close to her. Here he was stirring up a flurry of disruptive feelings inside her, and she had no affect on him at all.

Without meaning to, she blurted, "I'll never find another job as good as the one I lost."

Mace studied her. "You were really promoting concerts?" he asked finally.

Dale shrugged. "Concerts and other special events. It was hectic. There were always a million details. But I got to travel and meet people and have the satisfaction of bringing quality entertainment to people all over the world." Her expression grew animated. "The past three years just flew by."

"So what happened?"

"A lot of things. Basically, the owner lost interest in the business. His clients weren't getting the special attention from him they were accustomed to, and some started working with other promotion companies. It came down to a staff reduction. Harvey said he was drawing the line strictly by seniority. Maybe I should have seen it coming, but I was totally unprepared. He told me I'd always done a good job for him, but he figured his younger reps would have an easier time finding new jobs."

"Age discrimination in reverse. Unfortunately, he probably has a point."

"Well, searching for a job and not finding one is the most demeaning thing in the world. It's been months, and I'm still here with my grandparents."

"I thought sales jobs usually go begging for the right people."

"I had an exciting job where I could really challenge myself. I'm not going to start selling medical supplies or used cars."

"So, you're fickle."

"It wouldn't be fair to me or an employer to settle for less than what I want."

"I'm beginning to see the resemblance between you and your grandfather."

Dale shot up off the bench. "That was cruel."

"I didn't mean it to be, sorry."

"I just have standards."

''So does Sam, uncompromising standards.''

''I didn't come out here to discuss your differences with him. Nor burden you with my sad story. I truly didn't mean to unleash all that on you. I'm determined to get through this without wallowing in self-pity. Let's go back out to that baseball field I saw. Can we put a stage out there?''

''No problem. I can get you the names of some local musicians.''

''Thanks, but there's no need. Johnny Reading is coming.''

Mace stopped short. ''Johnny Reading is coming here?''

''Yes. That should bring in a crowd, don't you think?''

''This town will be swamped. Johnny Reading hasn't performed anywhere near here for years. People will be coming from other states. Dale, this town isn't equipped to handle that.''

''I'll take care of it,'' she assured him, studying his face and wondering if Gramps hadn't been right. ''You weren't wanting the festival to fail, were you?''

''Why would I? I just don't want want to see this town trampled. I think you should reconsider, Dale. How did you get him to come, anyway? You said last night most celebrities stay booked in advance and charge hefty fees. And I was thinking on a lesser scale than Johnny Reading.'' His eyes narrowed. ''How much is he costing us?''

''We'll have to pay his expenses, but those can come out of the money I'm not getting. Otherwise, he's appearing as a favor.''

''You just called him up and invited him.''

''Basically.''

Mace shook his head. ''You do move among the rich and famous. I can see why Meadowside bores you.''

''I worked with him on a tour, and we became friends,'' she explained curtly, anxious to change the subject. She hadn't brought up Johnny's name to impress anyone. She was proud of what she was doing for this sleepy little town.

Mace was staring at her. ''You are one for surprises,'' he noted.

''I don't mean to be mysterious. And I know my grandfather's attitude toward you makes you uncomfortable. I can see it every time the two of you are together. I apologize for that.''

''It's not your fault. You don't need to apologize.''

''Until recently, I haven't had the opportunity to spend much time with my grandparents. Gramps has gotten so used to having me underfoot, I think he was provoked that I was leaving this morning, especially with you.''

''Having your company is worth risking Sam's ire.''

She rolled her eyes. ''Don't let Gramps hear you talking like that. The last thing he wants is for us to become friends.''

''Imagine that,'' Mace said coolly. She had missed his point completely.

Chapter Four

But Dale had not missed his compliment.

Unsure how to react to it, she simply skirted over it.

Now, as they headed back toward town, she surreptitiously watched Mace as he drove and wondered what had prompted his comment. Was this ridiculous lightheadedness she felt in his presence less one-sided than she had believed?

He had a magnificent profile, his nose ended in a point as sharp as an arrowhead. Sunlight glittered in his hair as the wind tousled it. She liked his clear-cut looks and his aura of self-assurance. Probably some of the very traits that made Gramps distrust him.

He glanced sideways and caught her admiring him.

Quickly, she stiffened her expression. "I'll need the folders from the previous year's festivals," she reminded him.

Mace nodded. Still mulling over her abrupt dismissal of his earlier comment, he'd been startled to glimpse her warm, open appraisal, despite her attempt to mask it.

Obviously, she was determined to maintain her distance from him. His first guess was she was doing so out of loyalty to her grandfather. But he didn't figure Dale to be a woman who gauged her life according to anyone else's rules.

So why? He sensed she liked him. Boy, he sure felt something brewing whenever he got close to her. Didn't she feel anything?

She probably met so many people, she was careful about whom she aligned herself with.

Mace glanced up at the clear blue sky. He knew better than to get too deeply entangled in anyone else's life. Yet he liked how he felt when Dale was around. He wanted them to be friends, and he'd never been one to shy away from what he wanted.

"Yes, of course. We can run by my office and get them. But there's someplace else I want to take you first."

"Where's that?"

"Chamber of commerce office. You might get some help there."

"Great."

Mace tapped his fingers against the steering wheel. Something lingered on his mind. "You know, we probably will be spending a good deal of time together from now until this fiasco is over. I'm sure your grandfather has had an unflattering thing or two to say about me, and maybe we should clear the air. I mean, if you think I've been unfair to him or to the town, you should just come out and say so."

"There are two sides to every story. I form my own opinions."

"Oh."

"You don't seem to be the ogre Gramps makes you out to be."

"Thank you."

"You're welcome."

As they reached the three-block-long downtown area, he pulled the car up to the curb in front of a tiny white frame office building on one corner. Mace checked his watch.

"Good. We're in time. The office closes at noon," he said.

"It is almost lunch time, isn't it?" Dale asked, assaulted by the smell of food cooking in the diner across the street. Being out in the open air had spurred her appetite.

"Almost," he agreed, pulling open the office's front door and stepping aside for her to enter.

A pudgy young man in his late twenties, wearing a wrinkled white shirt with a multicolored geometric print tie was seated behind a scratched wooden desk, a telephone receiver pressed to one ear.

He nodded at them as they entered, signalling with an upraised index finger he was nearly finished with his phone conversation. Mace pulled two worn plastic chairs up to the desk, gesturing for her to sit down.

A few seconds later, the man behind the desk hung up the phone. His glance fell immediately on Dale.

"You must be Sam's granddaughter. I'm Jack Hall, laughingly referred to as the chamber director."

Dale accepted his handshake. "Nice to meet you. How did you know who I was?"

"Word travels fast around town. And before you start trying to back out, I want you to know how much we all appreciate your taking on the festival planning. It would be part of my job, but this is a bare bones operation. I'm only here half a day, and it's all I can do to keep up with routine business. But just holler if you need any help." He pointed to a rickety table in the corner. "You can set up a work station over there. This place is small, but I'm happy to share."

Inspecting the area he indicated, Dale frowned. "Is there at least a file cabinet?"

"I'll have a cabinet and desk brought over from the plant first thing tomorrow morning," Mace offered before Jack could answer. "We have some surplus office furniture in storage."

"Good," Jack agreed. He turned to Dale. "See, just ask and I'll take care of everything."

Dale laughed lightly. She liked Jack's easy sense of humor.

"A list of local contacts is the first thing I'll need."

Jack nodded. "I can give you a list of everything from the local historical society to the poetry club. And, of course, your grandfather's president of the model railroad club. But I've got to warn you, Dale. You may be disappointed when you start asking for volunteers. A lot of people in this community have gotten pretty complacent."

"I don't think she'll have any problem getting people involved this year," Mace piped up. "She's got something big up her sleeve. Although I have reservations about it."

"What's that?" Jack asked, his interest piqued.

Dale drew in a deep breath. "Johnny Reading's coming to sing."

Jack whistled. "When my wife hears that, she'll be the first in line to buy tickets. How did you manage that? Last I heard, he had stopped doing concerts after he got into the movies a few years ago."

"Well, this probably won't be a full-blown concert. He might sing for an hour if we're lucky."

Jack shook his head incredulously. "I have a feeling we'll have to get a lot of tickets printed."

"Meadowside's going to make some money this year," Dale reflected.

Jack looked up at Mace. "Let me be the first to put in my request. With some office help for the routine stuff, I might actually accomplish something."

Mace shifted in his chair. "I imagine we have a number of worthwhile projects going wanting. The council will have to designate which will benefit. What to do with the festival proceeds hasn't been an issue for the past several years, since there haven't been any."

Jack flashed Dale a smile. "I guess it was our lucky day when you came our way."

Mace set one hand on her shoulder. "Come on, I'll buy you lunch. This might be the last chance you get to take a break for the next six weeks."

"Lunch sounds good," Dale accepted.

"How about you Jack?" Mace invited.

Jack shook his head. "As soon as I'm done here, I have to get over to the shop and spell Joyce. Thanks anyway."

"I guess I'll be seeing you in the morning then," Dale told him. "Nice to meet you, Jack."

"Likewise."

"Is the diner all right?" Mace asked as they stepped

onto the sidewalk. "Homecooked food. Everything from scratch."

"It sounds like you eat there often."

Mace shrugged. "I'm not much of a cook."

"What shop was Jack talking about?"

"He and his wife moved here to open an upholstery and furniture refinishing business. They're picking up steam, but for now Jack needs to stabilize their income by working for the chamber too. I'm afraid we'll lose him pretty soon."

"Listen, it's nice of you to offer to pay, but I can afford to buy my own lunch. I'm not destitute yet."

He shook his head. "My idea, my treat. Why is it so hard for you to accept anything? I want to buy you lunch."

"Well, all right. I don't have trouble accepting things. I just thought you might have offered because you thought I didn't have any money."

"And when I said spending time with you was worth risking more of Sam's disapproval?"

She rolled her eyes sideways toward him. "I got the feeling you didn't consider my grandfather's opinion before acting on anything."

Jack shook his head. "See, that's where you're wrong. I would very much like to work with your grandfather, not against him. We both want what's best for the town. We just disagree over what that is. Your grandfather has earned the respect of everyone here. And then there's my reputation. Can you imagine what it's like to be known as the arch enemy of a war hero?''

Dale laughed appreciatively. He liked the way her face lit up.

''Somebody must have voted you into your council seat.''

Mace nodded. ''Sure, the younger people who want to see the town grow. Meadowside's becoming increasingly divided into two factions—those who want growth and those who want time to stand still.''

''So, the dilemma is to preserve the quaint, small-town atmosphere while keeping up with modern times to provide jobs so people can continue to live here.''

''Exactly. Does Sam know yet about Johnny Reading?''

''No. You're the first person I've told. Why?''

Mace shrugged. ''I just wonder what his reaction will be.''

''He'll be thrilled. The festival is one tradition he doesn't want to see fade away. Ensuring its success is the only thing that prompted me to ask Johnny to perform. This means so much to both my grandparents. They met at the festival.''

They stood in front of the diner's front window. ''Ah-ha,'' he proclaimed. ''You see there. You *are* a hopeless romantic, a starry-eyed dreamer.''

She shook her head. ''You misunderstand everything I say. These are my grandparents. If they hadn't met and gotten married, I wouldn't be standing here talking about all this. Fate is what you make it. I think you're the dreamer, spouting all this idealism about small town life. Peace, quiet, and fresh air.''

He looked down on her, shaking his head. ''No, I'm afraid my idealism was tarnished a long time ago.''

''You see. That's why it's so refreshing to look back on simpler times, when there was such a thing as 'happily ever after.' People were satisfied with so much less.''

Mace offered a smile. ''It's amazing to find someone whose logic meshes so closely with my own,'' he said.

''So how did your idealism get tarnished?''

''That is a long story I prefer not to tell.''

''Oh,'' she said, miffed by his sudden evasiveness.

Mace studied the pert young woman before him. Could someone so lovely really tackle life with such a straightforward approach? *Too bad she wouldn't sell used cars*, he thought. *She would probably make a fortune.*

And now he had shut her out by refusing to answer a perfectly natural question. But he wasn't going to dredge up a past that was best left buried.

He reached out and clasped the brim of her cap between two fingers, adjusting it slightly.

Dale felt the funniest sensation race through her, like high-voltage electricity.

"What are you doing?" she asked.

"This cap is turned up too high. It needs to be down some if you want to look like a baseball player." Impulsively, he wondered what it would feel like to lean down and kiss her. Of course he couldn't do that.

"I don't want to look like a ballplayer," she protested, stubbornly readjusting the cap and shaking her head. But she was still reeling as she entered the diner. She didn't believe in telepathy, but she didn't need any magical powers to have sensed he had wanted to kiss her a moment ago.

And that didn't upset her as much as her own disappointment that he hadn't.

Dale sat across from Mace in a corner booth. The food was every bit as good as he'd promised. She'd ordered the special—meat loaf, mashed potatoes and gravy, and green beans—while he had opted for a cheeseburger and waffle fries.

She managed to keep the conversation on business, asking questions about previous festivals. No point in probing into personal areas when he had made it clear those were off-limits.

Midway through lunch, Mace suddenly looked up, his brow furrowing as his attention was drawn to something across the room. Dale turned and followed his alarmed eyes.

On the opposite side of the diner, two women were at a booth, eating lunch and talking, not paying attention to the toddler who had unbuckled the strap on his high chair and was busily trying to stand up.

Mace tossed his sandwich down on the plate and flew across the room, catching the tot just as he was about to plummet to the floor.

The child's mother, who had seen too late what was about to happen, gasped with relief, gratefully taking him from Mace's arms.

"Thank you," the embarrassed woman said, clutching her son.

"No problem," Mace told her. "I'm just glad he's all right."

As Mace returned to the booth, the two women watched him, whispering.

Dale eyed him with a new admiration.

"Anyone would have done that," he said quickly. "I just happened to see what was going on."

"Lucky for that little boy," she said, sipping her cola through a straw.

"Believe me, I'm no hero."

"I wish my grandfather could have seen that."

"Really?"

Dale set her fork down. Somehow, before she left, she was going to get Mace and her grandfather working on the same side. Accomplishing that, however, might take a miracle.

She stirred the iced cola with her straw. His evasiveness disturbed her. Maybe if he was more open about his past, Gramps would stop drawing his own conclusions.

"So why did you leave Indianapolis?" she asked.

He winced. "Didn't you ask me that earlier?"

"No, I asked you why you came here."

"Indianapolis just wasn't working for me any more."

"Oh, come on, talk about vague."

"Well, there's no great mystery to it. I started my company in my garage. I'd reached a point where I needed to expand. All at once I realized there was nothing to keep me in Indianapolis. I could go anywhere. So I thought why not start fresh somewhere new?"

"Didn't you hate leaving your friends behind?"

"I still see my friends occasionally. And I've made new ones here."

"What about your family?"

He smiled slightly. "My parents still live in the house where I grew up. My brother and sister are both married and have families of their own. I see them all on holidays."

Dale looked down at the formica table top. "Sounds like you enjoyed a storybook childhood.

Gramps thinks you've run away from some sordid past.''

''To your grandfather, anyone whose past isn't right here in Meadowside has a dubious background. I prefer to think of my leaving as running *to* something rather than running away.''

Dale reluctantly let Mace pay the bill.

His plant was a low brick rectangular building located on the opposite end of town from the park.

''Come on inside,'' he urged as he parked alongside the building. ''This is something I don't mind showing off.''

During the next hour, Dale met nearly every employee in the factory and watched with fascination as they crafted hot metal from behind thick protective masks that made them look like spacemen.

She marveled at the intricate replicas of antique European chandeliers and Victorian lamps.

''Actually,'' Mace explained, ''the advent of electricity is so recent, you don't have many truly antique electric lamps. Most replicas are adaptations. People seem to like these.''

''Understandably so. These chandeliers must make your customers feel like royalty.''

''This all started kind of by accident. Someone asked me if I could duplicate a real antique her friend had. We also make candlesticks and candle trees.''

''Candle trees?'' she asked.

He found one and showed it to her, a tower of metal spiraled by individual candle holders. "You have to see it lit to fully appreciate it. Unfortunately, I don't have any candles here."

"Too bad. I'm sure it's magnificent."

"I'd better get those folders before I forget."

When they reached his office, Dale was surprised to see a slight, white-haired woman sitting behind a desk.

She sprang out of her chair the minute she spotted Mace approaching. "There you are," she said. "I've got a stack of phone messages for you as deep as a sinkhole."

This news didn't seem to disturb Mace. "Shelly, I'd like you to meet Dale Addison. Dale's taken charge of Meadowside's autumn festival."

Shelly nodded. "Good to meet you. Aren't you Sam Guthrie's granddaughter?"

Dale felt heat rise to her cheeks. Did everyone in this town know her?

"Yes, I am," she answered. "I didn't realize anyone knew I was here."

Shelly laughed. "In this dinky little town people speculate. We've all heard you were here, but we wondered why we never saw you. Sam never misses an opportunity to brag about his granddaughter."

Dale grew uncomfortable. Given her current situation, Gramps didn't have much to brag about now, she reflected. Who would want to hear about his unemployed granddaughter? She hadn't stopped to reflect she wasn't the only person disappointed by her layoff.

She offered a tentative smile. "Well, everyone can stop wondering now. Here I am."

Shelly studied her. "You look exactly like your mother."

"You knew my mother?" Dale asked, tensing.

"Sure. My husband and I, well he's dead now, used to run a little grocery store in town. As a teenager, your mom was always coming in there for magazines and paperbacks. She always had that kind of wistful look in her eyes. She was a dreamer, your mom. When your dad came along, I think she found the magic she was always reading about. The knight in shining armor and all that. How is your dad?"

Dale knew Shelly meant well, but she was only underscoring the tragedy of her mother's early death. She had left so much happiness behind her. Because Dale scarcely remembered her and knew she could always do all right on her own, she felt sorry not for herself, but for her mother and all the Christmases and anniversaries and quiet moments she had missed.

"He's all right. He's remarried now."

She didn't want to hear any more about her mother.

It was Mace who inadvertently saved her. "Ah, here they are," he proclaimed, holding up a handful of folders extracted from the cabinet he'd been digging in.

"Great," Dale said, more relieved at the diversion than his locating the folders. "I guess we'd better be going now. It was nice to meet you, Shelly."

When they were out in the parking lot, Mace asked, "Are you all right?"

"Sure. Why shouldn't I be?" Dale asked, puzzled, as she stepped into the car.

"Shelly's mention of your mother seemed to make you uncomfortable."

She was surprised he had noticed. She had thought his attention was focused on the files.

"It sounds odd to hear strangers talking about her," she explained. "My mother died when I was six. I scarcely remember her.

"I would think you'd be starved for details. Don't you want to know what she was like?"

Dale shook her head. "I don't want to carry around a collage of other people's recollections. None of them make her seem real to me."

He nodded solemnly. "I can understand that in a way," he said. Although he couldn't know completely how she felt—his own parents alive and vivid images in his mind—he sensed her confusion. She felt guilty because she wasn't eager to hear stories about her mother. He suppressed an urge to fold her into his arms and soothe her. The protective feelings she sparked surprised him. Dale certainly wasn't the type of woman who looked to anyone else for strength. And a long time had passed since anyone had made him feel this way.

Remembering how that last time had turned out, he didn't lean closer to her, as he had been about to do. "You want your own memory of her but you don't have one?" he surmised.

"Exactly," Dale concluded, eager to change the subject. "Shelly was kind of a surprise."

"A surprise?"

"Well, she looks around sixty."

"She's seventy, and the best secretary I've ever had. She couldn't make ends meet on Social Security, so she enrolled in a program where she could go back to school and learn to use a computer. She works about thirty hours a week, which is fine for me."

Once again, Dale found herself studying Mace's profile as he drove. This was the man her grandfather accused of wrecking the local economy? A man willing to hire a seventy-year-old secretary?

And again, he caught her looking.

He flashed her a smile that made her heart do a somersault.

Reflexively, she smiled back, aware of the warmth spinning between them. Something was going on here she didn't understand. She was well-practiced at establishing a rapport with even the most difficult of her clients and got along with most people. But this force tugging her toward him was beyond her control. While wild and a little thrilling, this roller coaster was also frightening.

"I've kept you away from your work this morning," she ventured.

"Being on the council, I have an obligation to the city too," he said. "Besides, I spend enough late nights at the office to make up for any time I'm away during the day. In fact, I'll probably be tied up until I go for a run in the park this evening. I'd be happy to pick you up if you'd like to join me."

He tried not to let her see he was holding his breath as he awaited her response.

Dale realized this invitation was strictly social.

And she liked being with Mace.

All she had to do was say yes.

She toyed with the cuff on her shirt sleeve.

She really didn't need a complication like this right now when her life was in ruins. She liked him more than she could handle. And if she agreed to see him, she might be stepping into a relationship she wasn't ready for.

"Thanks, but I have some things to do."

Mace didn't say anything, just nodded as he drove.

Inviting her to go running had seemed safe enough.

Just a few seconds ago, he had felt a connection to her, and she seemed to be retuning it.

Why then, had she turned him down flat? *Maybe she suspects just what a cad I really am.*

Chapter Five

Dale gleefully marked another check in the "yes" column she'd ruled off on the legal pad on the desk in front of her, giving Jack a thumbs-up sign.

On the other end of the phone line, Lila Markum's voice hummed. "I'll have to ask the other members, of course, but I believe the Happy Needleworkers will want to set up a booth at the festival. We hadn't made any plans yet because we'd nearly given up hope this year."

"We certainly will be having one," Dale assured her, looking up to see a long shadow from the front door of Jack's office. For a moment, she was nonplussed as she realized Mace was coming inside. "I'm looking forward to working with your group. And I can't wait to see all those handmade items."

"Well dear, we're meeting next Thursday at my house. Why don't you come and join the group?"

"Oh, I just admire other people's needlework. I don't know how to do any."

She looked up to see Mace's keen brown eyes fixed on her. Her heart began reeling in the all too familiar way it did when he was close by.

The friendly, chatty woman on the other end of the phone continued. "We have plenty of members who can teach you anything you want to learn—quilting, smocking. We even have a lady who tats. And honey, hardly anybody tats any more."

Dale felt the heat of Mace's eyes on her. "Well, I appreciate the invitation, but I'm tied up organizing this festival right now. Maybe another time."

"All right, dear. But if you change your mind, just come on. Anybody in town can tell you where my house is."

"Sure. Thank you, Mrs. Markum."

"I've been hearing something interesting around town. Is it true Johnny Reading's coming to our festival?"

"He'll be there."

"No kidding? Well, I'll have to call my daughter. She said she'll be driving her family in from Milwaukee if he's really coming."

"Terrific. It's going to be a great festival. Goodbye, Mrs. Markum."

She set the receiver in its cradle and looked up again, surprised at the unexpected harshness in Mace's expression.

"At least you gave her a rain check," he noted.

Confused at first, Dale realized he was referring to her rejection of his invitation yesterday.

Her eyes darted to where Jack sat behind his desk a few feet away. He tried unsuccessfully to pretend he wasn't listening—an impossible feat in the cramped office.

She straightened the papers she had scattered across the desk two of Mace's employees had delivered a few hours ago.

"I'm sorry," she said stiffly. "I wasn't trying to be discourteous."

"No, I'm out of line. I'm the one who should apologize. I didn't come here to start an argument. I came to make sure the desk and cabinet are adequate."

"They're perfect, thank you."

"Good. Now that that's out of the way, it's time for a coffee break."

Dale's mouth dropped open, and she was about to beg off when he held up a thermos suspended from one hand. "I even brought the coffee," he informed her.

Dale's lips curled into a soft smile. "Then how could I refuse?"

"My thoughts exactly. We can go over to the park beside city hall."

"I thought we could stay here."

"I'll bet you've been sitting at that desk all morning with the phone stuck in your ear. The walk will do you good."

She saw he wasn't going to back down no matter how much she protested, and she didn't want to make an even bigger scene in front of Jack.

"All right," she agreed. "But only for fifteen minutes. I have scads to do. Do you want us to leave you some coffee, Jack?"

The hefty man waved one hand. "No. I never touch the stuff."

She transferred his phone back to his desk.

When she and Mace were out on the sidewalk, Dale asked him, "Why do I suspect you knew Jack didn't drink coffee?"

"You should be flattered that someone would go to such lengths for your exclusive attention."

"I am. But that worries me too."

"Ah ha. That's what I want to know about. Is it me? I didn't mean to be so edgy back there, but it's been preying on my mind since yesterday."

A few weathered picnic tables, a flower garden, and a fish pond were wedged onto a treed lot beside the boxy red brick city hall building. Mace led her to one of the tables where he uncorked the thermos.

"I've brought an extra cup," he said, filling the thermos lid and handing it to her, then fishing a styrofoam cup from the pocket of his sport coat. "Sit," he prompted.

She complied. The steaming coffee was hot and good. Until now, she hadn't realized how much she did need a break from the confines of the dismal little office and the telephone.

"You didn't answer my question," he reminded her.

"I thought you'd forgotten. The answer is yes and no," she explained. "It's not that I don't like you, Mace. And although I wish you and my grandfather got along better, I wouldn't refuse to see you because of what he thought."

"Then tell me you turned me down because you don't like to run."

Dale emitted a soft laugh. "Sorry, I do like to run, although I'm afraid I've gotten out of shape. That wasn't my concern. The thing is, I've planned my life very carefully, and at this point I'm like a trolley off the track. I don't need any distractions. My main concern is getting back where I'm supposed to be."

"But the fact remains, you're here. I don't see any reason for you to avoid spending time with me. To be perfectly honest, I like being with you, Dale. In many ways, we think alike."

Dale eyed him helplessly. He had no intention, she

saw, of accepting even the most logical of explanations. And she couldn't very well tell him her normally level-headed way of thinking escaped her when he was around because her heart kept careening out of control and her knees got wobbly. No, she wouldn't give him a clue about that.

And she definitely wouldn't reveal that she could barely sleep last night because she kept seeing his face in her dreams and reliving that quivery feeling she'd gotten when he reached over to straighten her hat and she had known he wanted to kiss her. Had that simply been her imagination? She didn't think so.

But knowing how he made her feel, she couldn't casually agree to go out with him either. Those traitorous feelings were bound to surface sooner or later.

"My emotions are tangled up enough as it is," she told him.

"Then you're completely safe with me. I'm never getting involved in any kind of serious relationship."

Dale raised her eyebrows, wondering what pain he had endured that prompted a statement like that. Right now, her life revolved around her career, if she still had one. Marriage and a family loomed far in her future, but they were there. Someday, when the time was right, she would fall in love and settle down.

Moreover, from what she had seen of Mace, he cared too much about people to be the loner he was now claiming to be.

"Really? You should be careful about saying never," she cautioned him.

"I mean it."

"How can you be so sure?"

He shrugged. "I have a company to worry about, just like you're concerned with finding a job." She knew he was withholding the real reason. "Which is all the more reason we should go out. Neither of us will have to worry about the other getting some sentimental delusions."

"Heaven forbid." But she remembered what had happened with Johnny. Maybe Mace had a point. In the face of all his logic, she couldn't confess being with him made her uneasy because he set a nagging thrill coursing through her veins. "You've obviously thought this out thoroughly."

"I also thought dinner might be more appealing than running."

"Mace? You're not doing this just to spite my grandfather, are you?"

"No. I promise. I wouldn't. Believe it or not, I want to get along with your grandfather."

"All right. I can't see what harm one dinner would do."

He graced her with a broad, shining smile. "Tonight then."

"Tonight?"

"There's a country inn not far from here. The food's great."

Hesitantly, Dale returned his smile. She'd already learned he knew good food. But she had the unsettling feeling that somehow this simple, innocent dinner date was going to change her life forever.

Dale found Gramps in the basement, where he was racing his electric trains around a labyrinth of track permanently mounted and secured on a table-top.

She watched the miniature cars travel around curves and under bridges, a column of smoke spewing from the smokestack atop the locomotive.

"It's a tiny little world," she marveled, admiring the complex of model buildings, the train yard, the figures of people and animals.

Gramps huffed. "It's a nice place to get away to sometimes. I guess you think it's silly—an old man playing with toys."

"I love the trains."

"You did when you were little too." He handed her the controls.

Mildly surprised, she accepted them. "You were collecting them even back then. What if I crash the cars?" she asked.

"Then we'll have a mess on our hands, won't we?"

Delighted, she started the longest train crawling around the track.

"You never let me operate the train before," she noted.

Gramps shrugged. "You were just a little girl last time we saw you. You have to understand the gap is kind of hard to cope with. We knew you as a child, then didn't get to spend any time with you until you were grown. You'll have to excuse us while we get accustomed to your being an adult."

"The way things are, I feel almost like I've been reduced to a child. Without a job, I can't take care of myself. I shouldn't be imposing on you and Grandma."

"I don't want to hear any more about this 'imposing' business. In fact, we haven't seen much of you the past few days."

"Well, I've been working on the festival. At least that's keeping me busy. It feels good to have something to do beyond typing letters asking for a job. Ninety percent of them don't even draw the courtesy of a reply, and the others bring form letters that say 'Thanks, but we're not interested.' How can they know that without even talking to me?"

Gramps scratched his bristly jaw. He shook his head. "Those companies are the ones missing out. I don't understand how all this job changing works. After I got out of the Army, I went to work for the railroad and stayed there until I retired."

Dale watched the train duck under a tunnel. "I don't think my generation is going to enjoy that kind of security. I really felt I had a future at my company. Then wham, I have no job at all."

"Listen, if you need some money for your car payments or something. . . ."

"Oh, Gramps, no. If things get that bad, I'll flip hamburgers before I take your money. It's kind of you to offer, but I'll manage. You and Grandma are doing so much for me already."

"Let me know if you change your mind."

"I will," she assured him, although she had no intention of relenting.

"So how is the festival shaping up? Is this true what I hear about some hotshot movie star coming here?"

She nodded. "Johnny Reading. He's a singer actually. I wanted to tell you myself. The grapevine in this town works faster than network news."

"Well, Dale, you told the council we couldn't afford to hire a celebrity. And now one is coming. I don't understand."

"Johnny's a friend. He's coming here as a favor."

"A very good friend, I'd say, if he's bypassing all the money he could charge and coming to a place no one's ever heard of." He turned a stern glance to her, and she nearly did wreck the train. "Is this your boyfriend we should be expecting to meet?"

Dale's face turned purple. "Gramps, nowadays men

and women can be friends without some big romance
going on—''

''I don't want a treatise on modern society. Your
business is your business. But if you've fallen in love
with a movie star and he's coming here, I'd rather hear
about it from you than in the barbershop.''

''No,'' she assured him. ''I dated Johnny a few
times, but in the end, we're just friends. He's a real
down-to-earth guy.''

Gramps nodded thoughtfully. ''And tonight, what
are you so dressed up for?''

She took a deep breath, then blurted, ''I'm going to
dinner with Mace Travers. I know you don't like
him. . . .''

''But I'm not going out with him,'' he finished
calmly.

''You're not upset?''

''I think you could have chosen better. I don't trust
Travers. He doesn't keep his word.''

''You're talking about the workers he moved
here?''

Gramps nodded. ''Said he was going to hire all local people so we'd swing him a good deal on the
land.''

''He believes he did keep his word.'' Dale defended
Mace. ''The only people he brought in were those with
skills no one here had. He couldn't wait years to go
into production. He would have been bankrupt, and

none of the people who work for him now would have jobs."

"Sounds like he went to great lengths to persuade you he was right."

"I brought it up. I asked him why you and he were at odds."

"You know what they say about someone who protests too much."

She switched off the train and handed the controls back to Gramps. "He doesn't hold anything against you. I think you're just angry because someone new moved in here, and he's successful and has the respect of other people. He's brought new ideas along with him, and just imagine what the two of you could accomplish if you mixed those with all you know about this town and the people in it. Meadowside needs people like Mace. It can't stand still and survive. Why don't you give him a chance? He was willing to compromise on keeping the festival as long as it wasn't going to cost the town money."

Realizing she'd lost her temper with someone who had never been anything but good to her, she clasped a palm to her forehead and raced up the stairs. She hadn't meant to lecture Gramps. But she couldn't sit back and allow him to misjudge Mace.

When she reached the landing, she turned and headed back downstairs. Gramps was unplugging the train set.

She approached him. "I'm sorry, Gramps," she apologized. "I didn't mean to blow up. I've just had so much on my mind lately. I've been sending out millions of resumes without hearing anything and now I've taken on this festival. It's just that I like Mace, even though I know you don't, and I don't want him to feel uncomfortable when he comes over here."

Gramps looked thoughtful. "When I saw him here yesterday morning, I couldn't help remembering the first time your mother brought your father home."

"Oh, Gramps. It's not like that. We're just. . . ."

"Friends?" he finished for her.

"I know you can't help comparing me to my mom, but I wish you wouldn't. I don't remember her much."

He looked shocked, then his expression melted into a sad smile. "That's the problem. I remember her like she was here yesterday."

Dale gave her grandfather a hug. "I don't think I'm much like her."

"In some ways, you're exactly like her. Take my word for it. And if it means that much to you, I'll try to be more friendly to Mace. But keep in mind, I don't share your high opinion of him."

"Thank you, Gramps," she said.

She went back upstairs and stood in the bedroom that had once belonged to her mother. Closing her eyes, she groped for some sense of the woman she kept hearing so much about. Her father, she realized, never talked much about the wife he'd lost. The memories, she supposed, had been too painful for him. Or maybe he had been trying to forget so he could carry on with his life, dutifully raising her and eventually starting over with another marriage.

But standing here now, she felt nothing. Far back in her mind, she imagined a voice calling her name, a pleasant, lilting voice. But she was convinced that was more fabrication than memory. That part of her past was too distant. It remained a blank.

She told herself it didn't matter.

The doorbell rang, and she took a last look around the room before going downstairs to answer it. Sometimes things that should be important in life just slip away forever, she decided. And once they were lost, there was no getting them back.

Chapter Six

Mace thought Dale looked absolutely beautiful when she opened the door wearing a cream-colored knit dress splashed with a pattern of flowers. The hair that normally brushed her shoulders was swept dramatically atop her head.

But she wasn't smiling as she greeted him. He wondered what was wrong, whether she'd had second thoughts about accompanying him tonight.

Just as he was about to press the bouquet of flowers he held into her hand, Gerard came rushing to the door to welcome him.

"Down boy," Dale commanded, capturing the dog by the collar before he could lunge at Mace. "I thought you were outside. Well, you will go into the yard now.'' She started down the hall with him. ''Come on in,'' she called back to Mace.

Mace, who had hoped to avoid another encounter with Sam, was left standing at the door with no option but to step inside.

Hesitantly, he did so.

Hoping to linger in the foyer only a few seconds, he was crestfallen when Sam rounded the corner.

''Good evening, Mace,'' Sam addressed him with uncharacteristic cordiality.

''Evening, Sam,'' Mace replied, twisting the flowers in his hands. Maybe they were too much, he reflected. Enjoying good spirits this afternoon, he'd bought them impulsively.

''Come on in and sit down,'' the older man invited.

Immediately suspicious, Mace felt like the fly being invited into the parlor. What had come over Sam? Was this his secret, amiable double?

''Thank you,'' he said, following Sam inside. He walked over to the sofa and found a spot to wedge himself in between the mound of throw pillows. Where had Dale gone? She should have been back by now. Had Gerard dragged her out the door?

Sam grinned at Mace, increasing the younger man's discomfort. What was the old man up to?

''Can I get you something to drink?''

''No, thank you.''

Mace felt like he was back in high school, calling for his first date.

To his relief, Dale finally entered the room, Rachel trailing in behind her.

"Would you like something to drink, Mace?" the older woman offered.

"No, thanks. I'm not thirsty."

Actually, his throat was starting to get dry.

He remembered the flowers, stood, and presented them to Dale.

"You shouldn't have," Dale said, truly surprised by the gesture. Her hand tingled where he had brushed it with his. As she went to get a vase, Mace caught the same sentiment reflected in Sam's dark glare. So, this was really Sam here after all.

Sam quickly masked his displeasure, and Mace suddenly understood he was making an effort for his granddaughter's sake. Oddly, he felt a stab of kinship for the old man. Sam might be dead wrong most of the time, but he wanted to do the right thing, especially where his family and his neighbors were concerned.

Well, if Sam was making an effort, for whatever reason, Mace would meet him halfway. "I think you'll be pleased with the job Dale's doing on the festival," Mace told Sam. "People can't seem to volunteer fast enough."

Sam's eyes pivoted briefly to his granddaughter. "I

know I'm the one who spoke up in favor of continuing the festival, but now I'm wondering whether it's getting too big too fast. I've never seen people around here so excited about anything.''

Mace set a hand on one knee. He couldn't believe Sam was voicing a concern he shared.

''I think you're right, Sam.''

Stunned, Dale swung her glance between the two men. Here she'd wanted them to stop feuding, and when at last they agreed on an issue, it was to disapprove of her strategy.

''I don't believe in doing things halfway,'' she stated. ''I know you're both suggesting Johnny's appearance will bring in too big a crowd, but if I cancel it now that people are excited about it, you might as well call off the entire festival.''

Mace looked at Sam. ''She is right. It's too late to change course. Everyone's already expecting Johnny Reading.''

''Don't worry,'' Dale urged. ''I have everything under control. I've alerted hotels in all of the surrounding towns that reservations will be in demand the first weekend in October.''

She saw the strain in her grandfather's face and shot him a grateful look. She knew he was compromising his principles for her, but she hoped in the past few minutes he'd begun to see Mace as less of a threat than he imagined.

She turned to Mace. "We need to be going, don't we?"

Instantly, he was on his feet. "We do have reservations."

"Take an umbrella," Rachel advised as they were leaving. "The weather forecast says rain."

"There's not a cloud in sight, Grandma," Dale observed, peering through the front window.

Rachel tossed her hands in the air and shook her head. "Well, sometimes those weathermen are wrong. Have a nice time."

"Thanks. I'm sure we will," Dale replied, unaware of how wrong she was.

"How far away is the inn?" Dale asked as Mace guided the convertible over the winding country road. Dale's grandmother and her weatherman had not been so far off track after all. With amazing speed, dark clouds had gathered menacingly overhead.

"Not far," Mace assured her. "You'll like it. It's on a hill overlooking a lake."

"Sounds nice. I think I like it already." Right now, she needed to retreat to a quiet, pretty place.

The first raindrop splattered across the bridge of her nose.

"Oh boy," she said, holding a palm upraised to catch subsequent raindrops.

"Don't worry. I'll just put the top up."

He slowed the car, pressed a button on the dash, and the top began rising.

Dale sank back in the bucket seat.

"Let me ask you something," she said.

"Shoot."

"When you said this afternoon you were never going to fall in love, you were being dramatic, right? I understand what you meant. You meant not at this point in your life."

"No, I meant never."

"Sounds awfully bitter."

"Does it?"

"And I'll bet it has something to do with the reason you left Indianapolis."

"Now who's being dramatic?"

"Look out!"

Turning sharper than any roller coaster, the car swung toward the ditch to avoid the pair of headlights speeding toward them head-on. Dale felt herself being flung sideways, the seat belt digging into her flesh as it restrained her.

She heard a scream, unaware it was her own, as the car flipped onto its side and teetered there. Dale closed her eyes, furiously recanting a childhood prayer as she prepared to die. With a slam, the car fell upright.

Except for the patter of raindrops, the world was sickeningly silent.

Her heart threatening to explode, Dale didn't dare move.

"Dale? Dale, are you hurt?"

Mace was leaning over her, his voice frantic.

Oh, he must be all right.

Gradually, she took inventory. She was still breathing. "I think so."

Her stomach was in one big knot, and her vision was blurred. But she didn't feel any pain except soreness where the seat belt had gouged her.

Instead of relief, she felt suddenly cold and afraid, trembling uncontrollably.

"I don't know what that jerk was doing," Mace said. "He was going so fast, he must have swung over to our lane on that curve up ahead. And then he didn't even have the decency to stop."

"We could have been killed," Dale insisted indignantly. Her eyes flew to the crumpled metal. "Your car!"

Mace waved off that concern. "It can be fixed. Come on, let's go find some help."

Smelling gasoline, Dale reflected that on television wrecked cars always blew up and quickly stepped out. Anger gripped her. What if they'd been pinned in the car and unable to summon help on their own?

Despite the fact that she couldn't stop shaking, she didn't need any coaxing to get out of the car. She glanced up and down the deserted road. "Which way should we go?" she asked.

He pointed in the direction they had been travelling. "If I remember correctly, there are some houses not too far ahead."

Dale shivered. Her hose were already soaked from the wet grass, her high-heeled sandals offering little protection for her feet. Even though it was the end of August, the raindrops struck like ice pellets.

Walking by Mace's side, she headed down the road. And when he wrapped an arm around her shoulders and pulled her closer to his side, it felt like the most natural thing in the universe.

The rain sheeted over them. The storm had cloaked the scant, remaining evening light, and skirting the country highway without benefit of streetlights, Dale felt truly lost.

Mace, strong and unflinching at her side, was all that felt real to her. Her gratitude that he was unharmed drove home the depth of her feelings for him. In just a short time and without wanting to, she'd grown quite attached to him.

Right now, she was so grateful both of them had escaped from the accident unscathed, she didn't even care about being unemployed.

Surely a car would pass by soon. Even in her current predicament, she wouldn't get into a car with a stranger, but she would ask the driver to summon help.

"I guess we've lost our dinner reservations," she commented.

Mace's light laughter echoed in the night. "I'd forgotten all about them."

"No matter. My appetite seems to have vanished."

"I'm sorry. This was supposed to be a perfect evening."

"If you hadn't reacted as fast as you did, I'm afraid the results would have been much worse."

"This isn't going to set well with Sam."

"Mace, your car is totalled and we're wandering around out here getting drenched. My grandfather's reaction should be low on your list of concerns."

"Sorry. For a second there, earlier, I'd almost hoped the tension was easing between the two of us. Little chance of that now. He's very protective of you, in case you haven't noticed."

"I've noticed. I'm his only grandchild. My mother was still in her late teens when she left home and married my father. Because she died only a few years later, I don't think he ever got over that. It was the only thing in his life that didn't work out as it was supposed to. Unlike my life, fraught with chaos."

"You'll find a job soon. You're too good not to."

"Would you believe that at the moment I couldn't care less? But thanks for the vote of confidence. I wish you had as much in yourself."

"What's that supposed to mean?"

"Ohhh!" The heel of her sandal slipped on the gravel, throwing her off balance. Mace caught her as she fell against him.

Leaning into his grasp, she looked up at him briefly. A stirring so strong radiated through her that she had to shift her gaze. Her heart raced wildly.

"Are you all right?" he asked.

"Yes. But I've got to take these stupid shoes off before I trip and break a leg. They're not exactly keeping my feet dry."

He steadied her as she leaned down to remove the shoes.

"There," she concluded, rising with the shoes dangling by their straps from one hand.

The rain slowed slightly.

"Look," he observed. "Things are starting to go our way."

"At long last. I'd give about five hundred dollars for my grandmother's umbrella right now."

Mace glanced down at her. Tendrils of her carefully styled hair were plastered to her neck, water ran down her face in rivulets, and she was continually shivering in her wet dress.

He reflected guiltily that he'd insisted she come out with him tonight. Why couldn't he have left well enough alone? She would be safe and dry right now.

Wasn't it just his bad luck to find someone he cared about, only to have barely escaped with their lives from their first date.

Exactly how much he did care sneaked up on him. This was the first time he'd acknowledged it.

Something more was going on than just wanting to not eat another dinner alone. She felt good against him. Whenever she entered a room, it was as if all the lights had suddenly come on.

That his feelings ran this strong unnerved him. He had experienced something similar to this only once in his life. And that had been disaster. He'd promised himself then never to risk losing himself again. He had meant what he told Dale this afternoon. He didn't want any serious relationships—ever.

So why couldn't he stop feeling like he wanted to scoop her into his arms and hold her to his heart forever? Nothing in his experience had been this overwhelming.

He loosened his grip around her shoulders.

"You were saying something before about my confidence," he said to break the silence and the intensity of his own thoughts.

"Well, you seem perfectly confident about running your business and the city and rescuing falling infants. But then you say you're never going to find any happiness for yourself beyond that. That's a pretty bleak prophecy, isn't it? I mean, I'd take you for a person who was sure of making his life work all around."

"That's not exactly what I said. And you said the same thing about yourself."

"No. I said I wasn't concerned with complicating my life right now."

"After what you said, I thought you might relax a little knowing I wasn't out to sweep you off your feet. But I was telling the truth."

"Nobody can be so sure about that."

"Hey, when I first started my company, I had visions of becoming successful exactly so I could get married. Obviously, that didn't work out. Maybe there's no such thing as having it all."

"And now you're bitter."

"Just wiser."

Her voice was low against the backdrop of rain. "I'm sorry, Mace. Really. You must have been very disappointed."

"That's an understatement."

"What happened?"

"Kimberly and I grew up together. I know this will absolutely repulse you, but her family lived next door. All through high school we were off and on, sometimes dating, sometimes buddies. We talked about getting married someday, and I liked the idea. Both of us went away to college. Both of us moved back home. We dated, and talked about getting married, but she was going to graduate school at night in addition to working full time at her nursing job. I had an entry-level accounting job that bored me to fits, so I kept puttering in the garage at night. Once I made that first chandelier, things took off, and I spent most of my time building the business, while still working at my job during the day.

"I was in the garage one night, working, and she came over just glowing. She looked prettier than I'd ever seen her before and told me she was getting married. Just like that. Like she had forgotten the plans we made and expected me to be happy about it. You see, she'd changed while I wasn't paying attention. But I hadn't. That's when I knew I needed a change and came here."

"She couldn't help it if she didn't feel the same way you did any more."

"No. I never blamed her. I know it was my fault. I'm not capable of maintaining any kind of lasting relationship. I did everything wrong."

"And I can't keep a job. Maybe we are two of a kind."

"I don't think you should give up on yourself just yet."

"And I don't think you should either. Are you happy with your decision?"

Mace considered. He'd never expected seclusion to bring him happiness, only a refuge for his wounded spirit.

But he never got a chance to answer her.

She stopped suddenly in her tracks, her hand flying to his chest to halt him. "Look!" she instructed excitedly, pointing into the darkness up ahead.

Mace squinted. He saw the distant flicker of light in the darkness.

"It must be a house. Oh, please let the occupants be home."

Mace looked down at her, smiling encouragingly.

"I have a feeling they will be."

Dale beamed up at him. Like a gear slipping, the tenderness she felt for him stole over her. Without thinking, she sprang up on tiptoe, planting an impulsive kiss on his mouth.

Caught off-guard, Mace tasted lips cool and rain-laced as rose petals. His defenses vanished, and the powerful emotions he had been struggling so hard to repress, kicked in.

Dale suddenly realized what she'd done, but before she could retreat, his hands slid to her shoulders, pulling her closer, extending what had begun as a casual kiss into one deep and lingering.

Her resistance ebbed as warmth skyrocketed through her. The rain, the darkness, the craggy ground, and all else lost meaning to her as she yielded to the delicious swirling sensation he provoked. Even in the dampness, he smelled of spice.

When he drew back, she was rattled. How had this happened? It was wonderful, but not what either of them wanted.

"I didn't mean for that to happen," he said, finally. "Sorry."

Dale searched his eyes, trying to discern whether he really meant that, but she couldn't see them clearly in the darkness.

''It was my fault,'' she countered. ''Seems nothing either of us does works out as we intend it.''

Stooping, she stuffed her feet back into her shoes, then hurried toward the light they'd seen. Although Mace caught up with her, she did not stay close enough for him to put his arm around her.

Now, if only her foolish heart would return to earth, everything was going to be fine.

Chapter Seven

Dale stood huddled on the wooden porch of the square frame house, rubbing her cold hands together while Mace knocked on the front door.

An eternity passed before the porch light came on and the heavy door creaked open.

A white-haired woman eyed them warily from behind the screen, which she did not unlatch.

Mace flashed the most winning smile he could manage under the circumstances.

"Sorry to bother you," he told the woman. "We've been in an accident down the road. Could we use your phone?"

The solemn woman studied Mace. Then her eyes

shifted to Dale, who could only imagine what she must look like right now.

To Dale's distress, the door slammed shut.

"Call the police for us then!" she called after the woman, incredulous at her behavior.

What would they do now? She hadn't seen any other houses nearby.

"After this, I don't ever want to hear another person say New Yorkers are cold," she spouted. "So much for small-town compassion."

Mace, not knowing what else to try, was about to knock on the door again. Maybe if they refused to go away, the woman would call the law.

Just as he raised his fist, the door magically re-opened. This time a short, squarely built man with hair cut so short he looked bald stood in the door frame, his wife hovering over his shoulder.

"Got some trouble?" he asked, scanning the pair on his porch.

"My name is Mason Travers, and this is Dale Addison," Mace explained slowly. "We've been in an accident and we need to use a phone. If you could just make a call for us. . . ."

The man was unlatching the screen. "I know you, Mr. Travers. My son works for you. Come on in out of the rain. Is anybody hurt?"

Mace extended an arm and drew Dale to his side. "No. We're just wet and cold and shaken up."

The man held open the door. Dale hesitated before entering, remembering the woman's stony stare. Well, of course she'd be alarmed to find two soaking wet strangers on her doorstep. The poor woman had probably just been frightened.

When the woman made no protest as Mace entered, Dale followed him inside.

The tiny living room was neat and spotless, obviously furnished with great care. The walls were covered with family photographs, and lace curtains hung over the front window. A television set glowed in one corner.

Dale felt slightly better already.

"Come on in the kitchen," the man directed them. "Phone's in there."

The kitchen proved every bit as cozy as the rest of the house, gingham covering the windows, ivy and onions hanging in baskets, an aluminum tea kettle sitting on the stovetop.

The man left them alone with the phone while his wife filled the kettle and turned on the burner. By the time Mace was finished, cups of hot tea had been set in front of them.

Dale sipped hers gratefully. Nothing had ever tasted so good.

"Thank you so much," Mace told their hosts, holding his cup up in front of him before taking a drink.

The woman finally spoke. "You're welcome," she

said. "But you'll both catch pneumonia if you don't get out of those wet things. I'll see if I can find something for you to wear. My son left some clothes here."

"Oh, please don't bother," Dale insisted.

"Don't be silly," the woman said. "You're shaking like a leaf."

Dale looked at the cup in her hand and saw she was indeed still shaking.

Undaunted by Dale's protest, the woman turned and left the room. Her husband sat at the table with them.

"I'm Earnest Wilson," he told them.

"Robbie's dad." Mace replied. "Your son's a hard worker, Mr. Wilson."

The old man nodded. "Kind of high-spirited though. He'll settle down one of these days. He just left here a little while ago. I'm surprised he didn't pass you on the road."

"Hmm," Dale reflected. "All we saw was one green and white Pontiac."

Mace fell strangely silent.

"That was him," the man said.

Dale's eyes flew to Mace. She realized from his expression he was already aware that he knew the car.

She returned her attention to the old man. "That was the car that ran us off the road."

He nodded slowly, his head drooping. "I can't say I'm surprised. I've been telling him that wild driving is going to get him in trouble someday. Looks like someday's come.''

Dale patted the man's arm. ''I'm sorry,'' she said. ''We'll have to describe the car to the police. He could have killed someone.''

''I know what you have to do,'' he acknowledged. ''Just don't say anything in front of my wife. Let me tell her.''

As if on cue, the woman walked into the room, a pile of folded clothes topped by a thick bath towel on each arm. She handed one to Dale, one to Mace.

''We've only got one bathroom to change in,'' she apologized.

''Go on,'' Mace urged Dale.

A towel had never been such a luxury. Dale dried herself and put on clothes she suspected belonged to Robbie, jeans that were far too big for her and a gray T-shirt that swung over her like a tent. Still, they were dry and more comfortable than her own drenched clothes, which she deposited in a plastic trash bag Mrs. Wilson had given her.

Mace took his turn and reappeared in a pair of cut-offs and a T-shirt that barely fit.

Just as he stepped into the kitchen, there was a knock on the door, and the next few hours were a blur of statements and reports.

Earnest Wilson took them back to the accident scene to meet the sheriff's deputies. Dale stood by

Mace's side as the tow truck pulled his mangled car from the ditch.

All the while, she wanted to reach out and hold his hand. She suspected the car meant more to him than he admitted. But she held back, afraid of what he would read into it.

In the back of her mind, she couldn't help remembering the compelling tenderness of his kiss. She knew it would haunt her for a long time to come. What was happening to her? This was the wrong time, the wrong place, and most definitely the wrong man. When she did fall in love someday, it would be with someone willing to love her back.

Still, she wasn't sorry it had happened. She realized now she had been wondering almost since the moment she met Mace what his kiss would be like. And she hadn't been disappointed.

A sheriff's deputy drove them back to the Wilsons' house. Dale felt a tug when she saw Mrs. Wilson was crying. Her husband must have told her by now that their son caused the accident.

Mr. Wilson dropped a set of keys in Mace's hand. "You can take the station wagon out back," he offered. Doesn't look like much, but it runs good. Use it as long as you need it. From the looks of your car, it might be a while."

Mace winced. "Are you sure?" he asked.

The old man nodded.

"Thank you."

Guided by a floodlight at the back of the house, Dale and Mace made their way through knee-high weeds to where the car sat. The rain had let up, and the night was still, the air smelling fresh.

As promised, the beat-up station wagon wasn't much to look at, the fenders rusted and blue paint faded to gray. But the engine started the first time Mace tried it, purring smoothly.

"Amazing," he said.

"I feel awful about their son. Will you fire him?"

"I don't know. I'll think it over when I'm less furious."

Her eyes widened. "You're furious right now? I never could have guessed. You've seemed so calm all night."

"Blowing up doesn't accomplish anything."

Dale sat back in the seat. "You're so good at covering the way you feel. I bet Kimberly thought you'd lost interest in her. That's why she fell in love with someone else."

Mace rolled his eyes. "Why do I know I'm going to regret having told you that? Look, it was a moment of weakness. I didn't think we'd ever get off that roadway. I'd appreciate it if you'd just forget it now. Why do you have to analyze everything?"

"My friends and I do it all the time. It helps put life in perspective. Besides, you're still letting it bother you."

"So you miss your friends and you're going to pick my life to shreds."

"It just saddens me that you've canceled a major portion of your life just because it didn't work out one certain way." She raised her chin. "I don't believe in looking back."

"I had planned to marry Kimberly for a very long time."

"Did you love her?"

"Of course I did."

"But you didn't say, 'I loved Kimberly for a very long time.' Maybe you weren't really in love with her either. I'd think it would be hard to tell with somebody you've known forever."

Mace shook his head. "Okay, if it will make you quit, I might get married someday far in the distant future. How's that?"

"Better."

He glanced sideways at her. "Besides, the past makes us what we are. Maybe in not looking back, you're avoiding feelings that make you uncomfortable."

"Is that so awful? Why dwell on disappointments?" Uncomfortable that the subject had shifted to her, she quickly added. "I'm starving."

"Shall we head for the inn?"

Dale glanced at their unorthodox dress and giggled. "I think the management would appreciate it if we didn't."

"Agreed."

"But I promised you dinner. And I intend to deliver."

"How? I don't want anyone to see me dressed like this."

"You won't have to. Trust me."

Still skeptical, Dale sank into the seat and gazed out the window. Suddenly she realized how much she wanted to trust him, and in a way that had nothing to do with dinner.

As the station wagon pulled up to the curb in front of the Guthries' brick bungalow, a pizza box balanced on the seat between Dale and Mace, Dale was surprised to see her grandfather sitting on the porch.

Immediately on his feet and moving quickly, he had reached the sidewalk by the time she was out of the car.

"Are you all right, Dale?" he asked.

"I'm fine," she assured him, reaching into the car for the garbage sack that held their wet clothes. "How did you know what happened?"

"Calvin Shepherd called me. He's got a scanner."

The old man's eyes leveled on Mace, who had just emerged from the driver's seat.

Dale braced herself, dreading the confrontation she knew was coming. Now, her grandfather was counting one more strike against Mace.

But her grandfather again surprised her. "You all right, Mace?" he asked.

Mace's eyes betrayed his own astonishment. "Yes, sir. I'm fine."

Dale watched her grandfather warily. As Sam digested the information and nodded slowly, she realized he was not acting for her benefit as he had been earlier. Somewhere deep inside, he was concerned about Mace's well-being.

Like a log catching fire, the truth snapped inside her. Her grandfather actually liked Mace, in his own begrudging way. Even though the two were constantly at odds, Gramps couldn't help admiring a man who stood up for what he believed in.

And Gramps couldn't blame Mace for the accident. He knew better. He knew Mace was responsible and careful.

Impulsively, she hugged her grandfather. "I'm sorry to have worried you. Thanks to Mace's quick thinking, we're both all right, but I'm afraid his car didn't fare so well. We did get wet, walking to find help. The people who let us use their phone lent us these clothes."

Sam appraised their appearance. "You'd better get inside. The two of you look like a couple of clowns in those getups."

Mace, glancing down at his attire, chuckled softly. "I have to agree with you there, Sam," he admitted.

By now, Rachel was standing on the front porch, one hand clutching her chest. "Oh, you're all right?" she called. "We've been so worried. Where did you get that car?"

"They haven't eaten yet, Rachel," Sam told her. "Let them have their pizza, then they can explain."

Sam ushered them inside. Rachel relieved Dale of the sackful of clothes, taking them to the laundry room in the basement.

Mace set the pizza box on the dining room table.

Dale sat down and helped herself to a slice. At least her hands were no longer shaking. Still, she knew she would remember the horror of the accident for a long time.

In a single instant when she might have lost everything, she had gained a clear vision of what was most important in life. As long as she and Mace were all right, she could cope with whatever else life handed her.

Now, pizza had never tasted so good to her. She reveled in the thick, gooey mozzarella and spicy pepperoni. At this moment, sitting in her grandparents' dining room with them and Mace was enough for her.

The rest of her life would work itself out.

She glanced across the table at Mace. He smiled at her with his eyes, and she felt a fierce tug on her heart. Was she losing it to him? Or had she already?

Not as hungry as she'd believed she was, she set

the remainder of her slice of pizza on her plate and sighed heavily. "What a night," she concluded. "I don't know what else could happen that hasn't already."

As if in answer, the phone rang.

"I'll get it," Rachel volunteered, wiping her hands on a dishrag as she headed for the kitchen.

She was back in a few seconds. "It's for you, Dale."

Wondering who would be calling her now, Dale raised her eyebrows and shrugged. "Excuse me," she said, going to the kitchen.

Johnny's voice greeted her when she lifted the receiver and said hello.

"Hey, Cowgirl."

She couldn't help smiling. She'd never known anyone as unfailingly cheerful as Johnny.

"Hi, Johnny. Please don't tell me you're calling to beg off the festival. This whole town is in a frenzy anticipating your appearance."

"You know me better than that. I was calling to check on the progress of your job search."

She raked fingers through her hair. "Bad subject. Not well at all."

"Well, don't worry. There's a public relations agency here that's interested in you. Intensely interested."

Her brow furrowed. "What's going on, Johnny?"

"Well, I've told them about you, and they want to fly you out to Los Angeles for an interview. How's your schedule look next week?"

"Well, I. . . ." Her mind was whirling. A job interview in California? She had hoped to return to New York, but that prospect looked slimmer every day.

Her hands were shaking again.

"I thought you'd be ecstatic."

She combed her hair with her hand again. "I am, Johnny. You just caught me off-guard. I was in a wreck this evening."

Concern overtook his previously light tone. "Good grief, why didn't you say something? How bad was it?"

"Not as serious as it could have been. I'm okay. My brain's a little rattled right now is all."

"Talk about bad timing. Do you want me to call you back tomorrow?"

"No. It's good to hear your voice, really."

"I wanted to tip you off about this job interview. A man named Bennett Rollins will be calling you."

"You set all this up for me?" she asked.

"It's not without some self interest. My agent sometimes contracts this agency. And it would mean having you living on the same coast with me."

Dale lowered her voice. "Maybe it will be easier for us to stay friends if I don't," she qualified. Johnny was one of the best friends she had ever had. And maybe better friends because of the distance between them. She didn't want to give him the idea she could ever think of him as anything more. She'd already gone through the agony of sorting that out with him once.

Johnny ignored her meaning. ''You'll love it out here. I have a hunch this interview won't be much more than a formality. And I think you'll like the agency better too. I know it's not exactly what you were used to, I told them if anyone can make people into stars it's you. Get in on the ground floor here and the sky's the limit.''

Dale rubbed a hand on her neck. ''I appreciate your recommendation, but I'm in the middle of planning the festival. There's not much time.''

Her glance drifted through the doorway where Mace was leaning back in one of her grandmother's antique oak chairs, his eyes dancing as he listened intently to one of Rachel's stories. Even in his borrowed clothing, he maintained that determined aura she found so fascinating.

Johnny's voice on the line interrupted her thoughts. ''Dale? This is Dale Addison, isn't it? Listen, let the hicks work out the apple-bobbing schedule themselves. This is everything you've wanted. I know you're anxious to be on your feet again.''

''They're not hicks,'' she defended the citizenry of Meadowside. No one here had been anything but kind to her, and she refused to look down on people because they chose a slower paced lifestyle than her own. But Johnny was right. She couldn't risk losing the job opportunity of a lifetime because of a volunteer assignment. She would just have to work harder once she got back. She would only lose two or three days at the most.

She swallowed hard and closed her eyes.

Johnny grew apologetic. "Sorry. I wasn't trying to belittle your grandparents and their neighbors, really. I just don't understand your hesitation. I thought you'd be on the next plane out here."

She smiled softly. She knew she should be wild with excitement right now. Why was she suddenly so reluctant to leave Meadowside?

"I'll be on the plane as soon as Mr. Rollins tells me when," she vouched. "It's just been a while since I've felt like I had a family, and leaving my grandparents is going to be hard."

"Understandable. But in any event, you can't stay there. For a second there I was wondering if they hadn't introduced you to the minister's son or something."

Her eyes flashed to Mace again. He and Rachel and Sam were laughing over something together. That was a welcome sight.

"No," she said quickly. "Of course I can't stay here. They haven't introduced me to anyone. Come on, Johnny, you know I'm more ambitious than that."

"Well, I'm getting anxious to visit this mysterious little burg that has captivated you. Listen, call me as soon as you know what flight you'll be on. I'll have someone pick you up at the airport."

She understood why he couldn't meet her himself. He would be mobbed by his fans. "Thanks, Johnny . . . for everything."

"Don't mention it. Just move here."

"We'll see what happens. Bye."

She hung up the receiver slowly. Johnny was so good to her. She wished she could have been what he was looking for. Nothing had ever been as painful as when she'd had to admit she wasn't in love with him, couldn't marry him.

For all his success, he was looking for something solid and stable. For some reason he had seen that in her. He had told her he was in love with her, but she knew she didn't love him that way.

She was glad they had remained friends. Now, she didn't want to revive any awkward situation. Johnny said he accepted what she'd told him, yet she wasn't totally convinced he wasn't still hoping she would change her mind.

Thoughts churning in her mind, she returned to the dining room.

"What's wrong?" Rachel asked upon seeing her taut expression.

"Nothing, really. That was Johnny. He's arranged

an interview for me with a firm in Los Angeles next week.''

Silence spun through the room.

''There goes the festival,'' her grandfather said finally.

Dale turned wide eyes to him. Preserving the festival for her grandparents had become nearly as important to her as building her own future. She couldn't have explained why.

''I'm not backing out on it,'' she promised. ''I'll only be gone a day or two. Surely things can't get out of hand in that short a span.''

Her grandmother turned to Sam. ''We knew from the start Dale would be leaving sooner or later. Look at her, a young woman with her whole life ahead of her. You didn't expect her to stay in Meadowside indefinitely, did you?''

Dale blanched, uncomfortable with being talked about as though she wasn't there.

''I haven't gotten the job yet,'' she reminded them.

''But I'm sure Johnny Reading's recommendation goes a long way,'' Mace cut in, his voice low and even. ''This sounds like exactly what you've been hoping for, Dale. I can keep tabs on the festival plans while you're gone.''

Dale stared at him, touched by his offer. In spite of that, she suspected she might have felt better if he sounded a little less anxious for her to go.

Her disappointment was her own fault. Hadn't he warned her from the start he wasn't looking for a lasting relationship? And at the time she had counted his independence as a point in his favor.

She avoided his eyes, fearing what hers might reveal to him. ''Thanks. I'll go check the dryer and see if your clothes are ready.''

Chapter Eight

Dale's eyes fluttered shut in relief as the wheels of the airplane touched down and she was back in Indiana again. Strange, how this felt so much like home in such a short time. In a way, it seemed as though she had lived here forever.

The past three days had been a blur. Sandwiched between the parties and outings Johnny had arranged for her, the interview had become the most indistinct memory of all. She'd met a parade of celebrities and Johnny's other friends, visited people she already knew, watched jugglers and banjo players perform on the street and sampled West Coast seafood.

She'd begun feeling more like her old self. Johnny, reassuring her his only motive was friendship, had been a gracious host, escorting her personally as much as he could, winning her over to the charms of sunny California.

Exhausted, she was happy to be home.

The plane seemed to approach the gate in slow motion.

Retrieving her carry-on bag from the overhead rack, she waited until the other passengers were off the plane before she tried to get off. She supposed she'd have to rent a car to drive back to Meadowside. It was too far to have expected Gramps to come for her, and Mace had dropped her off, so her car wasn't in the lot.

Absently, she bit her lip. Mace. In the midst of the whirlwind, he had constantly crept into her thoughts. Strange, she reflected, that she should miss him. Ever since the night of the accident, he'd been mysteriously aloof. He came over nearly every night to see her, but he hadn't kissed her again. He hadn't so much as held her hand.

She reminded herself she had initiated that kiss on the road. But he was the one who had continued it.

Despite the sparks she'd felt, the fact remained—he said he had never wanted it to happen at all.

Her confusion over his actions was her own fault. She couldn't expect him to care about her. Especially not now.

When she stepped through the gate, she was startled to see him standing there.

"Mace!" she greeted him happily.

Her surprise increased when he opened his arms, folding her into a warm embrace.

Oh, she thought, nonplussed as she basked in his caress, *I am home.*

Then she remembered how dangerous that kind of thinking was.

But he looked, smelled and felt so darn good. She couldn't help allowing her feelings to cave in just a little. She was road weary and tired of denying the exhilaration that swept through her in his presence.

It was something she was going to have to continue denying, though. For her own good as well as his.

"It's great to see you," he whispered in her ear, holding her tight for a long happy moment.

Dale struggled to keep from saying what popped into her mind, that he was the finest sight she'd seen in the last three days. She knew she was tired and vulnerable right now. Besides, she'd be leaving for good soon. Why make it any more difficult than it had to be?

"How did you know what flight I was coming in on?" she asked.

"I called your grandparents."

"Well, I appreciate it. I'm looking forward to not having to drive."

He raised one eyebrow. "Wild time in California?"

"I'll tell you all about it on the way to Meadowside."

She halted midway to the luggage pickup.

"Tell me you're not still in the station wagon."

He laughed lightly. "No."

After learning his car could be salvaged, Mace had tried to rent a loaner while the repairs were underway so he could return Earnest Wilson's station wagon. The old man had nixed Mace's suggestion, insisting he keep the station wagon until his own car was repaired.

Knowing Mr. Wilson felt responsible for what had happened even though it wasn't his fault, to keep him happy, Mace had hung on to the station wagon, scooting around town in the raggedy old car.

"I'm driving Sam's car today," he assured her.

She shifted the shoulder strap on her bag. "My grandfather entrusted you with the Cadillac? He won't even let me drive it!"

Sam's decade-old white Cadillac, kept shining clean and waxed, was his pride and joy.

She couldn't believe Gramps' dramatic turnabout where Mace was concerned. Almost as if now he wanted her to fall in love with Mace. . . .

She cut the thought short. Her grandfather didn't want her to go, she knew. And deep inside, she hated to leave him or her grandmother.

Why was she getting so sentimental? After all, she would be here until after the festival, and she could come back to visit. Now that she'd gotten reacquainted with her mother's parents, she wouldn't hesitate to come for holidays. If there was time to get away.

Gramps had been keyed in to her attraction to Mace from the start. Would he really go so far as to push her toward a man he claimed to dislike, believing doing so would somehow keep her here? He should know better.

She sighed. These questions were too weighty for her to muddle through right now. She needed to have a long talk with Gramps. But later. She was too tired to think clearly.

Mace carried her suitcase as they waited for the shuttle to the parking lot.

"Did you have a good time?" he asked.

"I did. Any problems with the festival plans?"

"Everything seems to be going smoothly," he reported. "But I am glad you're back to take that over again. I didn't realize how much the fall festival means to so many people here. You're certainly giving them something to remember."

"I do appreciate your keeping an eye on things for me."

"What are friends for?"

The van arrived, cutting short their conversation.

Mace glanced sideways at Dale as he drove. Her head was turned at an angle as she gazed out the window at the passing countryside. Unaware of him, she wore a relaxed expression, the corners of her mouth upturned in a glad-to-be-home smile. He wondered what was going through her mind.

Sunlight filtering through the car windows highlighted the brown hair that cascaded over her shoulders, and those long lashes laced her alert blue eyes. When he looked at those eyes, he thought of a calm tropical bay.

He had been unprepared for the wave of tenderness that crested inside him when she'd stepped off the plane. She was such a welcome sight, he'd been unable to maintain his resolve to keep his distance. Sweeping her into his arms had seemed the most natural thing to do at the moment.

And she had felt so good, smelling faintly of wildflowers and shampoo. Three days without her had been torture. How would he endure her leaving?

While she'd been away, he'd had time to think about it. No matter what else he was doing, thoughts of her invaded his concentration. After that one poignant and memorable kiss, he'd been jolted by how much he felt for her. He hadn't intended for this to happen. And she had made it clear where her future was headed.

Ever since he'd arrived in Meadowside, he had considered himself to be getting over Kimberly. And he'd thrown himself into his work to avoid thinking about it. Now, he acknowledged he'd been using Kimberly as an excuse to concentrate exclusively on his work.

He'd convinced himself marriage and a family wasn't what he wanted after all. But that premise had never been put to a test until now.

And he didn't know how to retract it without Dale suspecting he'd lied to her from the outset. Besides, Dale had made her position clear. He knew she had been perfectly honest about her intention to put her career first, to leave Meadowside. He didn't know how to persuade her to do otherwise. And he cared too much about her to try. There was nothing for her here.

At the airport three days ago, not knowing what else to do, he had wished her luck and watched her board the airplane. But that was lip-service only. He knew he should be rooting for her happiness, but in his selfishness he'd secretly hoped she wouldn't get the job. Now, he felt guilty about that. He should have wanted what was best for her.

Her glance shifted, and she caught him studying her. The blue eyes darkened. Again, he wondered what she was thinking.

"I won't be offended if you'd like to doze off," he said to break the silence.

Her lips curled into a smile. "Thanks, but I'm too excited to sleep. I brought you something."

"Oh?"

She reached for her carry-on bag on the floor and fished out a T-shirt. Proudly, she unfolded it to display the design.

"Thank you," he said. "I'm surprised you thought so much about me in the midst of all that glitz and glamour."

"The glamour grates after a while. Too many people pretending to be what they're not. And being with Johnny, it's easy to get lost in the shadows. That's one reason, well. . . ."

"Go on."

She hesitated. "One reason I wouldn't marry him."

Mace nearly ran Sam's cherished Caddy into a ditch.

"Johnny Reading asked you to marry him?"

She rubbed a palm against her skirt. "It was a long time ago."

"I don't think too many women would pass that up."

"Yeah, well, he's not really the self-assured superstar you see on television. Johnny grew up poor and neglected, pretty much in charge of a younger brother and sister. He triumphed over his circumstances, but he's looking for security. I don't know why he thought I could provide that. I'm certainly not a homebody. I admire Johnny. He's a good-hearted person. We're still good friends. He understands."

"You're sure of that?"

"Of course."

"For someone from New York, you're certainly naive. Hasn't it crossed your mind he wants you close by because he hasn't accepted your refusal?"

Dale raised a startled brow. "Okay, I was a little skeptical at first. But if that was the case, Johnny would have said or done something to indicate that during the past few days. Nothing like that happened. We were just buddies."

Mace scratched his jaw. "I suppose it's none of my business anyway."

"It's no secret."

"Well, I still don't accept Johnny's motives. And you've made such a difference here in such a short time. Everybody's buzzing about the festival. You've revived that old-time sense of community here. And even Sam is less grumpy these days."

"You're overlooking the important point that I have no job here. You wouldn't be trying to make me feel guilty, would you?"

"Me?"

"Well, you're doing one whopper of a job."

"Speaking of jobs, I guess you'd better go ahead and give me the bad news. Did you get it?"

A few silent moments passed before she answered.

"Yes, I did."

"How long do you have to let them know whether you're taking it?"

"I've already accepted it."

Mace's chest constricted.

He swallowed hard, managing a weak smile to mask the disappointment that speared him.

Finally, he spoke, nearly strangling on the single word he uttered, "Congratulations."

"Mrs. Markum, I can't possibly change your booth assignment with the festival only a week away," Dale explained into the telephone receiver, struggling to keep her voice calm. She tapped a pencil eraser on the desktop.

"Well, it's not me, you understand," Lila Markum's voice came back at her. "Some of the other Happy Needleworkers expressed concern about our booth being so far away from the entrance. The Sewing Circle and the hospital volunteers are going to be out in the open while we're tucked away in the back. At least that's what the other members told me."

"Visitors will be walking up and down the path. You're right next to the food booths, and people are sure to congregate there. Believe me, you can assure your friends it's a great spot."

Undaunted, the older woman continued. "Couldn't you just switch us with the Sewing Circle, dear? We were one of the first groups to sign up."

"Mrs. Markum, I can't do that." Dale flashed exasperated eyes at Jack. He smiled sympathetically and shook his head.

"I'd hate for our group to have to cancel."

Dale couldn't believe the woman was threatening her. She wouldn't give in to coercion, but the Happy

Needleworkers were already listed on the fliers and posters. And she wanted to avoid creating any bad feelings among the townspeople.

"It would be a shame for your group to miss a fundraising opportunity like this," she agreed. She remembered the woman's earlier invitation, and a sudden thought struck her. "Have you seen the festival layout?"

"Well, no."

"Maybe if you saw the overview of the grounds, you'd realize that your location will be a hub of activity. Are you going to be home for the next half hour?"

"Yes."

"May I come over and show you the sketch?"

"Oh, would you do that?"

"Yes, I'd be happy to. Tell me where you live."

She jotted down the directions the woman gave her.

"I'll be there in a few minutes," she promised.

"I'll put the tea kettle on."

"Thank you, but I won't have time for—"

A click on the other end of the line cut her off.

She stared at the receiver. "Why are people who were so cooperative a few weeks ago balking now?" she asked Jack.

"Was that Lila Markum?"

"Yes."

"She wants some special attention. My guess is if

you go over and have tea with her, any spot you stick the Needlecrafters in will be just dandy.''

''Like I have time for tea parties.''

''Some people here don't understand the meaning of not having time.''

''Well, listen, I hate to jump ship, but can you take my messages? I'm waiting for another quote on the pumpkins. So far, they've all been sky high.''

Jack nodded. ''Must be a bad pumpkin year.''

Dale placed her hands on her hips, suddenly remembering something. ''Weren't you supposed to go home about three hours ago?''

''The festival's generated a flood of inquiries to the chamber.''

''Oh, Jack, I'm sorry. I know you have your shop to run.''

''We've got some part-time help. It's really okay, Dale. Don't worry about it.''

She slung her purse over her shoulder. ''Looks like I've created a mess not only for myself, but for the whole town. Now the council members are arguing over what to use the proceeds for.''

''Funding for a full-time chamber director,'' Jack quipped. Then he grew serious. ''You know Dale, with business at the shop picking up the way it has, I expect to be out of here by the first of the year. If this does grow into a full-time job, I'd be glad to recommend you as my replacement.''

"Thanks, Jack. I appreciate your confidence in me, but I've already accepted the job in Los Angeles. I'll be leaving the day after the festival."

"I knew that. I just wanted you to know you have an alternative, in case you decided to stay here."

She shook her head. "I don't think so. I hate leaving my grandparents, but the job I've accepted is one I can really grow with."

"This small-town stuff is a little boring, hmm?"

"Meadowside's a nice place. I like it here. But I need something I can sink my heart into. It's different for you, you have your own business here. I don't think I'd be happy with a job that was going to be the same day after day."

Jack shrugged. "Well, count me among the many citizens of Meadowside who will be sorry to see you go. And your mention of the city council jogs my memory. Mace Travers was in here looking for you earlier."

Dale froze. She hadn't seen much of Mace since the day he brought her back from the airport.

"What did he want?"

"He didn't say. He stopped by early this morning when you went across the street to get coffee."

"Why didn't he wait? I was only gone a few minutes."

"Dale, I told him you would be right back. Don't get riled with me, I'm just the messenger."

"I'm sorry, Jack. I've got too many things on my mind at once. It's making me edgy."

"Why don't you do something relaxing tonight—rent yourself a good movie or take a long walk? Believe me, this festival is coming together. From my vantage point, I can see it happening."

"Thanks Jack, maybe I'll do that."

She didn't want to admit she was more concerned over Mace's avoiding her recently than the festival plans. She knew she could iron out those details. But her feelings for Mace were an aspect of her life she couldn't control. Why had he come by today?

And now she had reduced herself to being less than honest with him. She should have confessed her feelings. But why, when nothing could ever come of them? First off, Mace didn't want her to care so intensely about him. He would think she'd been misleading him from the start. But she'd never intended to get so entangled in his charms.

And Mace had based his life here in Meadowside, where there was no future for her. She couldn't see any way around that. Maybe that's why she'd been so quick to accept the job in California.

She'd expected her anticipation to increase as the date for her to leave neared. Once she had explained she'd taken charge of the festival as a temporary assignment, her new boss agreed to delay starting at his agency. Intentionally, she'd neglected to mention she wasn't being paid. No sense giving him the impression she was crazy, which she must be.

Actually, except for the snags, she was enjoying pulling the details of the festival together. Because she stayed so busy, her remaining time here was flying by. And while at first she had dreamed of recreating the magical kind of old-time harvest fair that had drawn her grandparents together so many years ago, as the festival date neared, she felt only a dull sense of resignation.

She was surprised to find Lila Markum's house only a few blocks from where her grandparents lived, very near the spot where she'd wrestled Gerard to the ground the day she met Mace.

The memory prompted a smile as she guided the Grand Am to the curb. What a sight she must have been! She marveled that Mace had even attempted to help her. But by now, she knew Mace well enough to understand he would have stopped to help anyone in trouble—a hobo or a princess.

She missed Mace now. Was she going to be able to leave him behind so easily?

No sense dwelling on the impossible. She had no choice. She couldn't just stay here indefinitely with no job, no sense of purpose, no income. She had to be realistic. Besides, it seemed Mace had already left her behind. If he cared about her as much as his kiss had indicated, he wouldn't have stayed away from her these past few weeks.

Funny, she thought. She'd poured so much energy into planning the festival, and now she dreaded it actually taking place. Everything would be so final then. This part of her life would be over. A month ago she had been frustrated because she had believed nothing was happening in her life. But this hadn't been such a terrible interlude. She had gotten to know her grandparents, to treasure them. And she had met Mace, who had awakened new, rich feelings inside her.

Mrs. Markum was waiting for her with steaming mint tea and a plate of homemade banana nut bread. As reluctant as Dale had been to come here, she found the simple refreshments food for the soul. Sitting on the sofa in Mrs. Markum's living room, decorated in dark shades of rose and strewn with doilies, rag rugs, needlepoint pillows and other handmade creations, she unwound. Except for the ticking of the cuckoo clock, it was peaceful here.

Mrs. Markum, thin as a matchstick with permed hair as white as cotton, gave scant attention to the sketch Dale unrolled before her. She preferred to tell tales of her years as city secretary before she retired.

"My husband, Arthur, retired the same time I did, but he never could adjust to it. He went to work part time at the chandelier factory. He had only been working there a few months when he got sick. He had to quit. He died about a year ago. But you know, honey, that young Mr. Travers who owns the company still comes over here at least once a month offering to run errands or make repairs around the house—whatever I need.''

So that's what Mace had been doing in this neighborhood the day of Gerard's squirrel escapade.

Dale wiped her hands on Mrs. Markum's embroidered white linen napkin.

''That's very thoughtful of him,'' she noted.

''Isn't it though?'' The older woman leaned closer and said conspiratorially. ''Have you met him? He's extremely good looking. Single too.''

Dale felt she would scream if she heard Mace's name one more time.

''Yes, I have met him. Listen, Mrs. Markum, I've enjoyed talking to you, but if you agree with me about your booth space now that you've seen the plans, I have a lot left to do today.''

''Certainly, dear. You come back, now. We'd love to have you join us at one of our meetings. There's nothing like working a needle to take your mind off your troubles.''

''I'm sorry. I won't be able to, Mrs. Markum. I'll be leaving town after the festival to start a new job.''

''Oh.'' The woman's smile dropped. ''That is a shame.''

By the time Dale left, it was too late to return to the office. She was close to home, but she didn't feel like going there either.

Remembering Jack's advice about relaxing, she considered treating her grandparents to a movie. She could afford to splurge now that she had a job in the offing.

But she was too restless to be comfortable in the confines of a theater.

The problem was Mace. Nothing seemed to banish him completely from her mind. For her own satisfaction, she needed to resolve things with him once and for all, even if it required putting her heart on the line, toppling the fragile balance of their relationship.

She turned her car down the road leading to his factory.

Chapter Nine

T he first thing Dale noticed when she pulled into the parking lot was Robbie Wilson's car. Just seeing it gave her a shiver.

Quickly diverting her attention, she was pleased to spot Mace's patched Corvette in its usual spot beside the building. So, he'd finally gotten it back.

The sunny September day had faded to a gloomy gray as swollen clouds gathered overhead. She smelled rain in the air.

Before entering the building, she mustered her resolve. What kind of reception Mace might give her, she had no idea.

When she walked into his office, she found him

standing over Shelly's desk, going over some papers with her.

"Well, hello, Dale!" Shelly welcomed her brightly.

Mace's startled expression was a tight mask.

"Hello, Shelly. Hello, Mace," Dale replied evenly.

"This is unexpected," Mace said finally.

Dale began questioning the wisdom of coming here. He seemed less than delighted to see her. But no, she had business to get straight with him. It was too late to back down now.

"Jack mentioned you'd come by the office earlier. I was out this way, so I decided to see what you wanted," she lied, hating that she felt the need to.

Mace seemed at a loss for words.

"Coffee, Dale?" Shelly offered, ending the silence.

"No, thanks," Dale declined.

Shelly's glance shifted from her boss to Dale, then back again. She grabbed a sheaf of papers from a basket on her desk. "I have to take these work orders to the back shop," she excused herself. "Good to see you, Dale."

"Take your time, Shelly," Mace requested, his eyes locked on Dale.

Shelly closed the door on her way out.

Dale and Mace stood eye-to-eye.

"I hope I didn't interrupt anything important," Dale apologized.

"No," Mace assured her. "We were just about to shut down for the day."

He was dressed casually today in slacks, a plaid shirt, and a caramel-colored sport coat that set off his hair and eyes. The sight of him sparked a keen longing in her heart. By now, she recognized that feeling for what it was. For all her rationalizing and careful planning, she'd fallen in love with the guy.

And that was what had drawn her here this afternoon.

Now that she was alone with him face-to-face, her heart was hammering.

"So, why did you come by?" she asked again.

Mace opened his mouth as if to speak, then closed it suddenly as if he'd thought the better of it. He stepped closer, and she caught the scent of his spicy aftershave.

Standing so near to him, she felt her heart swing into high gear.

Then wordlessly and wonderfully, he placed his hands on her shoulders and drew her closer.

Dale thought she must be dreaming. She looked into his eyes and saw something she'd been searching for all her life.

Slowly, he leaned down and kissed her as tenuously as a child takes his first taste of cotton candy. Dale closed her eyes, savoring his nearness, his touch, drifting into the magic that enveloped her.

After a long moment, he drew back, studying her glowing face.

"I'm not apologizing for that one," he qualified. "If you must know, that's why I came to see you. I've missed you, Dale."

"Mace, we both know you've been avoiding me. If I've done something wrong, I wish you'd just tell me what it is."

"No, Dale. You haven't done anything wrong. I'm afraid I have." His eyes flew to the office door. "Look, this isn't the best place to talk. Shelly will come barreling through that door any minute. Can we go somewhere?"

"All right. Neutral territory. The park?"

"Fine. Can you go now?"

"Yes," she agreed. "I have my car. I'll meet you there."

"Okay. At the bleachers on the baseball field."

She took a last look at Mace, fearing that once she walked out of the office she would discover what had just happened had been merely a dream.

"I'll see you there," he promised, offering a heart-stopping smile.

"Okay. Oh, and Mace. . . ."

"Hmm?"

"There was no need to apologize, either time."

He grinned. "Thanks for telling me that."

She flashed him a smile, then shrugged. "What are friends for?" she asked.

* * *

Since the route to the park took her almost directly past her grandparent's house, she decided at the last minute to stop and change out of her suit into a comfortable pair of jeans and a knit top.

The aroma of spiced meat and vegetables wafting from the kitchen was nearly irresistible. How comforting it was to come home on a dark afternoon to a cozy, warm house and smell dinner on the stove, she reflected.

"What are you cooking, Grandma?" she asked Rachel on her way out. "It smells heavenly."

"It's nothing fancy—just stew and rolls," Rachel downplayed her culinary skills. "I finally coaxed Mildred Honeycutt to hand over her stew recipe. But I know her well enough to suspect she's left out at least one key ingredient, so I made a few variations." She looked at her granddaughter in her change of clothes, the car keys dangling in her hand. "You are going to be here for dinner, aren't you?"

"Sure. Would you mind if I invited Mace? Is there enough?"

Sam appeared from out of the hallway. "Your grandmother always makes enough to feed a summer camp full of kids," he volunteered. "That's a good idea, bringing Mace to dinner."

Dale shifted her stance to one side. It seemed the time had come for that talk with Gramps she'd been postponing. "I thought you didn't like Mace, Gramps. Why the sudden change of heart?"

Her grandfather stiffened. "I thought you wanted me to like him."

"I do. I like Mace. But my liking him is separate from my plans to leave."

He nodded solemnly. "I'm sorry you're unhappy here, honey."

Dale could have screamed. Why was he doing this to her, twisting everything she said? "I'm not unhappy here. How could I be? I have you and Grandma, and everyone's nice. The countryside is beautiful and the air smells clean. I don't think I've ever had this feeling before, that I belonged somewhere. But I'm totally useless here. Don't you see, having a challenging job is about even more than making money and being self-sufficient. I need to know I'm making my little mark on the world, giving something to society."

Rachel glanced up at Sam. "She's young, Sam," she reminded him. "We've got to let her go on and live her life."

Dale cast her grandmother a grateful glance.

But Sam only snorted. "Building up the egos of movie stars. That'll improve the world all right."

Stinging, Dale raked a hand through her hair, pushing it away from her forehead.

"It's what I do," she retorted. "And it does seem to have made a difference in this comatose little town. What are all those projects you and the other council members want to fund with the festival proceeds?"

She stormed out the front door, stopping on the porch as she realized she'd lost her temper with her grandfather. She regretted it, but darn if he didn't have a way of understanding only what he wanted to understand.

Inside, Rachel shot a furious glance at her husband, nudging his arm.

"Oh, all right," he grumbled, shuffling toward the front door.

Dale heard the screen slam shut behind her.

She turned and faced her grandfather.

"I don't want to fight with you," she confessed.

"I don't want to fight either. I know how much your work means to you. Used to be only men felt that way about their jobs."

Dale smiled. "Only men were supposed to. Thank goodness it's the nineties. I doubt I would have fit in very well in the old days."

"I know you're determined to go, but that doesn't mean I have to like it. I was figuring you and Mace seem so taken with each other, if the two of you were to get married. . . ."

Her face was as red as a Christmas stocking. "There's no chance of that. Gramps, I couldn't stay here with you and Grandma or with anyone else and just do nothing."

"Maybe you could just stay here for a while and decide what you really want to do. You're not underfoot. No reason for you to take the first job that comes along.''

''It's a really good job, Gramps. I'd be foolish to turn it down.''

''You didn't seem too excited when you got back from California. You haven't seemed excited about it at all.''

''I've been too busy with the festival to really think about it.''

His look grew stern. ''Well, maybe you should think about it. Make sure you're not making a mistake.''

''You said yourself there weren't any jobs here for someone with my qualifications.''

''Who says opportunity has to be staring you right in the face? If you really wanted to stay, you'd find a way.''

''That's not fair!'' she shot back. ''Gramps, I love you and Grandama. I really do. And if losing my old job meant having a chance to get to know the two of you, maybe it was a godsend in disguise. You two are the only family I have left really. I know you were disappointed because my mother left, but I can't make up for that. I'm not her. I don't even remember her.''

Immediately upon seeing Gramp's wounded expression, she regretted her words. And she couldn't help wondering whether his obstinacy hadn't been part of what had driven her mother away. She was grateful she'd maintained enough control to keep that thought to herself.

Gramps turned toward the house, then stopped and looked back at her. When he spoke, he sounded beaten. "I've said what I needed to say. You bring Mace to dinner."

Mace. Dale gasped as she remembered Mace was waiting for her at the baseball field. How long had he been waiting? Or had he left, thinking by now she wasn't going to show.

Despite her panic, she didn't want to leave her grandfather on bad terms either. "All right," she agreed. "I guess we both need some time to cool down. I'll see you later, Gramps."

He nodded.

Still, she hesitated. "You know, if she had stayed here it wouldn't have changed anything. She would have still gotten sick. Only we wouldn't be standing here arguing now, because I never would have been born."

"Honey, I'm old enough to understand certain things are meant to be. I just have a feeling your going to California isn't one of them."

Dale watched her grandfather and shook her head. "But you were wrong about my mom leaving too," she reminded him gently.

After he went inside, she raced to her car, wondering why her world was suddenly unraveling.

* * *

Relief washed over Dale as she spotted Mace's car in the lot by the park. She pulled up beside it, getting out of her car and racing toward the baseball field.

A misty rain had begun to fall. Dale shielded her eyes with one hand and recognized his lean silhouette. He was sitting on the bleachers staring at the field as if a game were in progress.

He turned toward her as she approached.

"I didn't mean to keep you waiting," she blurted, sweeping a shock of damp hair off her face. "I stopped at the house to change and got caught in a confrontation with Gramps. He can be so darn contrary—"

Mace silenced her with a kiss.

"Slow down," he advised, smiling down at her and making her heart reel. "What has your grandfather done to get you so upset?"

"Making me feel guilty about leaving. And doing a good job of it, I might add. I mean, he knew from the start I was only coming here temporarily. My grandmother understands."

"You're determined to take the job in California?"

"Of course. I've already committed myself."

"You've got to do what's best for you. In time, Sam and everyone else will accept that."

"I just don't want to spend the rest of my time here fighting with him about it."

"Understandably. Are you sure you're not just getting defensive because Sam struck on a truth you don't want to admit?"

She couldn't believe Mace was siding with her grandfather.

"That I feel bad about leaving? Of course I do. Until I came here, I hadn't seen my grandparents since I was a little girl. In a way, I can understand why my father didn't take me to see them. He had his hands full working and raising me. And he and Sam had never gotten along well. I'm sure that was worse without my mom around to smooth things over. And my grandparents would probably sooner venture through the gates of hell than venture into New York City. But they never gave up calling and sending letters. When I lost my job, my own father didn't offer any help, but Gramps called right away and invited me to come here for as long as I needed to stay. As best as I can remember, I've never lived in a home like theirs, full of memories and love and odd little customs and collections. I suppose I'll always consider this my real home."

"But you had a home with your dad."

"Not like this. Our housekeeper was very efficient, but very regimented. My dad and I were close, I thought, but he never looked back. He either locked up or threw away all traces of my mother. There were none of her things, no photographs around the apartment. It's hard to explain."

"You never asked about her?"

"Whenever I did, he tensed up and sidestepped my questions. I guess eventually, I stopped asking. Anyway, I hate leaving my grandparents, but I can't go back in time, looking for some security I missed as a child. I suppose in today's world, my upbringing is more common than yours with your family."

"Maybe someday you'll have the kind of home you want."

"Maybe. Maybe not. I guess I'm worried that something might happen to my grandparents after I leave. If one of them got sick, I don't think they'd even let me know, thinking they were sparing me the worry."

"I could check on them for you. Sam seems to tolerate me better these days."

"Would you?"

He nodded. "I'd be glad to. I'd call you the moment I sensed anything was wrong."

"That would take one worry off my mind."

"What are your others?"

"I didn't mean necessarily that there were others, Mace."

"But there are, aren't there? For someone who had just gotten her dream job, you're not exactly jumping for joy."

She shrugged. "New job jitters."

Mace's intense look made her uneasy. He wasn't buying that.

She sighed heavily. "The job sounds great. My old job was great. I'm just wondering what if I move all the way out to California, put in a few years with this agency, and the same thing happens. It's really not like me to be pessimistic, and it's not that I lack confidence in myself. But I did my old job well, and that didn't save me from getting sacked."

"There are a lot of people out of work these days who feel victimized. Uncertainty is something everyone has to live with these days. There are no guarantees."

"I know that. Gramps has this feeling I shouldn't go."

"Sam? Having premonitions?"

"Don't laugh. He has this uncanny knack of picking up on things where I'm concerned."

"And he's usually right?"

She skirted that question. "If I don't take this, I'll be compromising myself."

"We didn't come out here to talk about your grandfather."

"I know. You were going to explain why you've been acting like I have bubonic plague."

"Because I feel like an idiot. I made a big deal out of explaining how I wasn't looking for any emotional entanglements. I thought since we were on even terms, there'd be no harm in the two of us spending time together."

"But something has happened neither of us anticipated, hasn't it?" she asked.

"You know?"

"Of course I know. It's happened to me too."

"I was afraid if you guessed how I felt, you'd think
I was the world's biggest liar."

"How could I when I was experiencing the same
thing? I never meant to start caring about you."

"After the accident, when I thought I might have
found you only to lose you. . . ."

"It was the accident that made it impossible to ig-
nore each other. Once we'd been through that together. . . ."

"No, I think it was that kiss. Oh geeze, Dale, I've
been unable to stop thinking about you since I first
saw you grappling with that dog of Sam's. That's what
I wanted to tell you today. I thought if I stayed away,
I'd get used to the thought of your leaving. Then it
occurred to me I was a fool for letting you go without
telling you how I felt."

Dale beamed at him. "I came to your office to do
the same thing."

Still, she felt something leaden in her heart. They
were both so carefully avoiding that word, "love."
And he wasn't asking her to stay. While she knew she
couldn't even if he had, she wanted desperately to
know he wanted her to.

Fickle, fickle, fickle. Obviously, her brains were

scrambled. Maybe he wasn't asking because he didn't want to make her feel guilty, the way Gramps had. Or maybe a part of him still belonged to Kimberly and his shattered dream.

But at least she had told him how she felt. She was relieved to be free of that secret. And most of all, she knew he held some degree of affection for her. Could she hope for more?

"You're invited for dinner. Grandma's homemade stew and rolls," she informed him.

"I'm not going to be in the middle of a battle between you and Sam, am I?"

"No, we've settled things for now."

"Then I accept. I want to spend as much time with you as possible before you leave. Is that all right with you?"

She favored him with a smile. "There's nothing I'd like more," she answered, meaning it with all her essence.

He took her slim hand and sandwiched it between both of his. Dale felt a powerful current run through her.

"I really don't want to go back just yet," she said. At the moment nothing existed beyond this rain spattered baseball field and the enchantment of having discovered love where she'd least expected it.

Right now she could have waltzed on clouds without falling through. Everything outside was bound to intrude eventually, but she wanted to preserve this joy as long as she could.

''Let's walk, if you don't mind the rain,'' he suggested.

She suspended a palm in the air. ''Call this rain?'' she asked. ''I've hiked through much worse.''

''Don't remind me.''

He released her hand, then wrapped an arm around her shoulders and drew her close as they walked through the park. Dale rested her head against his chest, thinking how strong and good he felt. How good it would be if she could always feel free to lean against him when she needed to, to be close by for him.

She knew she was dreaming, but it was difficult not to while she was blanketed in his warmth. He inspired her vision, and she indulged in it.

The park closed in on them, holding off the rest of the world. She wished this time would never end.

Chapter Ten

Night had fallen by the time Dale drove up to her grandparents' house, arriving a few minutes ahead of Mace. Her walk with him in the park had revived her spirits. Now, a warm contentment had settled over her. She refused to think about the day she'd have to leave him behind.

Suddenly, anything seemed possible. She believed in the strength of the bond between them. Tonight, they'd taken the first step in acknowledging it. Maybe life today didn't work as it had long ago when two people shared one dance then spent the rest of their lives loving each other. But somehow, everything would work out. Even if all she was meant to have was a lifelong bittersweet memory of these last few days in Meadowside.

An unfamiliar mid-size car was occupying her usual space in the driveway. Puzzled, she parked in the street. The car must belong to one of her grandparents' friends she hadn't met yet, although she saw what she thought must be a rental sticker on the back. Well, there was no reason her grandparents wouldn't know people from out of town.

But they would have told her if they were expecting company, she mused. Suddenly the clues fit together— the nondescript rental car, the unannounced arrival. There was only one person she knew who traveled incognito.

She bounded out of the car and up the walkway, to the astonishment of Mace, who had just pulled up across the street.

Unaware of him, she rushed inside the house without looking back.

She was not disappointed. Her hunch had been correct. Johnny, looking completely at home, was seated in the living room between her attentive grandparents. Clad in boots, jeans, and a black silk shirt unbuttoned at the collar, he was leaning back in the armchair perfectly at ease. Blue eyes sparkled beneath the trademark shock of dark hair swept across his forehead. The Guthries had immediately set to pampering him, making him feel at home. A glass of iced ginger ale fizzed on the end table beside him.

"Johnny!" she exclaimed.

He was on his feet at once. "At last," he said, gathering her into a hug. "I thought I'd come a few days early so you could introduce me to the wonders of rural life."

"Oh, Johnny, why didn't you call? How long have you been here? I'm so busy with the festival plans."

"I've already offered to show him around, while you're working," Sam volunteered.

Dale looked from Sam to the younger man, wondering how the unlikely pair would fare together. She wondered whether her grandfather realized this was one of the so-called egocentric stars he'd derided earlier.

There was a timid knock on the front door.

At once, Dale remembered Mace.

Johnny's expression tightened. "Are you expecting someone?" he asked. "I don't want anyone to know I'm here."

Dale nodded understandingly. "It's a friend I invited to dinner," she explained.

"Mace is like family," Sam added generously.

Dale's eyes flashed to her grandfather.

"He's not going to tell anyone you're here," Dale assured Johnny, heading for the door.

She opened it to find Mace standing on the porch looking befuddled.

"Something wrong?" he asked.

"No. Why?"

"You raced across the street like the house was on fire," he reported.

Dale laughed lightly. "Johnny's here," she said, keeping her voice low as if neighbors were lurking in the bushes hoping to overhear this news. "Come on in and meet him."

Mace balked.

"Come on," she urged. "I know you'll like him."

Reluctantly, Mace stepped inside. His frown indicated he was not one of Johnny's fans.

In the living room, she introduced the two men. Despite her effervescent tone, they faced each other like opponents preparing to duel, eyeing each other suspiciously.

Finally, Mace offered his hand. They shook hands politely.

Dale wondered why two of the people she cared most about in the world bore each other such instant hostility.

This was going to be a long evening. She was glad to see Johnny and wanted to hear his stories from the West Coast. But she also longed to be close to Mace.

She remembered Mace's earlier speculation that Johnny was carrying a torch for her. Maybe now that Johnny was here, she could prove to Mace she and Johnny were friends, nothing more.

Uncomfortable with the tension bristling in the living room, she happily volunteered to set the table and help her grandmother serve dinner.

The good, hot food improved everyone's mood. But Dale couldn't help noticing Mace shied away from the steady exchange of conversation between her, her grandparents, and the singer.

Over slabs of her grandmother's apple pie, Sam challenged Mace to a game of chess.

But Rachel quickly vetoed that idea. "Who wants to watch you two contemplate a chess board?" she asked. "I'll get out the Monopoly game so everyone can play."

Dale glanced over at Johnny, watching for signs of condescension. But he looked perfectly serious as he said, "That's something I haven't done in a long time."

Mace folded his arms across his chest. "Neither have I," he echoed.

Because Dale's mind wasn't on the game, she was the first to go broke. Once out of the game, she sat alone in the living room, listening to the spirited battle over Boardwalk underway in the dining room.

She was so deep in thought, she didn't hear Johnny come up behind her.

"Attention shoppers!" He imitated a voice talking over the loudspeaker at a discount store.

Her reverie broken, Dale laughed lightly.

"Everything going all right?" he asked.

She nodded. "Sure. It's great that you're here."

"Well, I'm bankrupt and finished for the night as far as Monopoly goes. And I'm afraid I'm zapped. It's been a tough day. I'm going to go on back to my place. Thank your grandparents for tonight for me, okay? I'll see you tomorrow."

"The chamber of commerce office downtown is the best place to find me. You're staying at a hotel? Is that a good idea?"

"I brought a bodyguard with me. Maybe that was a mistake. It was all I could do to keep him from tagging along tonight, until I reminded him I sign his paychecks and he needs only to accompany me at my request.

"And we're not at a hotel. Actually, it's a hunting lodge outside town. Peaceful, quiet and reeking of nature. Jack somebody at the chamber of commerce told my agent about it."

"Jack Hall."

"Anyway, I can actually appreciate the charm of this place. I'm sorry I made fun of it. Maybe I'll retire and settle down in a town like this someday."

"I believe you're serious."

"Why not?" He leaned over. "I am half-asleep on my feet to be babbling like this. Goodnight, Cowgirl." He brushed a kiss across her cheek.

Dale glanced up to see Mace standing in the doorway, scowling.

"Nice meeting you, Johnny," he said with false joviality.

Suddenly aware of Mace's presence, Johnny straightened.

"Same here," he returned and quickly made his exit.

Dale followed him to the door. When he was gone, she turned to Mace.

"I hope you see you were wrong about him," she told him.

"That's not what I see at all."

She lowered her voice. "Mace, I don't want Johnny's being here to ruin these few days we have left together."

"I don't want that either."

She returned his gaze evenly.

"I have to be going," he said. "Tomorrow's a work day."

"I'll walk you to your car."

"I was hoping you would." Finally, he sounded like himself again.

She waited on the porch as he said goodnight to her grandparents.

When he came outside, she told him she had noticed Robbie's car in the parking lot at the factory.

Mace grew thoughtful. "I told him what I thought of his recklessness, how much destruction he could have caused. I think he's learned his lesson, and the court will decide his punishment. I believe he's regretting what he did and deserves a second chance. I couldn't see any point in firing him.''

''Even when he didn't stop?''

''He turned himself in to the police a few hours later. He claims he panicked when he recognized my car. I'm giving him the benefit of the doubt that it was a mistake he won't make again.''

''Few people would have bypassed the opportunity for retaliation.''

''I'd like to think that's not true.''

''I know you would. How can you be so tolerant of everyone and yet make such quick judgments about Johnny?''

Mace stepped off the porch. She walked beside him.

''You're blind to the way he was looking at you all night. I'm telling you, it's more than friendship that brought him here. He's not being up front with you. He's using the guise of friendship to stay close to you.''

Dale studied Mace. He had never stuck her as the type of man who would be insecure or jealous without reason.

''Once you're in California, I say within a year he'll have convinced you to marry him.''

''I've already told you I have no intention of marrying him.''

''Maybe you don't. But I'm sure he can be very

persuasive. Maybe it wouldn't be such a bad thing for you if you did.''

He struck a tender chord. She clutched a hand to her sternum. "That's cruel!" she blurted. "You're the one I'm in love with!''

Horrified at her inadvertent admission, she raised her hand to cover her open mouth, backing away from him.

Mace's expression was a kaleidoscope.

"No," he coaxed, reaching toward her. "Don't run from it. And for heaven's sake, don't apologize.''

Dale stopped, and all at once she was in his arms. "I love you too," he murmured, holding her tightly. "I didn't want to say it. I was afraid it would complicate things.''

Dale didn't know whether to laugh or cry. "Things already are complicated," she pointed out.

"And this changes nothing, is that right?''

She nodded slowly, her throat tight. Nothing except her whole life. She would never be the same again. And she would never stop loving him, even if they were planets away. She didn't know if she was strong enough to walk away and leave him behind.

Mace sat in his car with the motor turned off, staring at the looming structure in front of him. Even under the faint moonlight, the house begged for repair—the exterior paint faded to a dull brown, the windows boarded.

Talk about a white elephant. Struck by impulse, he'd bought the place at an auction shortly after he'd moved here. Despite years of neglect, it remained structurally sound, and the price was too good to resist.

Ever since he was a boy, he had enjoyed working with his hands, taking things that were broken and making them whole again. He had intended to do much of the work on this house himself, then move into it.

The project, as anticipated, would fill his free time. As it turned out, he never had had any free time. Eventually, he realized he would be lost rattling around inside a three-story house. Still, he couldn't shake his vision of how it would look with fresh white paint, smoke curling out of the chimney and shrubbery lining the sprawling yard.

Resting his arm on the door frame of his car, he tried to figure out what had brought him here tonight. After leaving Dale, he had been reluctant to go home.

Only a few more days, and she'd be gone forever.

And he needed her in his life as much as he needed air to breathe. Could he just do nothing and let her fly away forever?

He closed his eyes, inhaling the sweet, damp, night air. He wanted her to spend the rest of her life with him. Not just as a fellow resident of Meadowside, but as his wife.

He hadn't intended to fall in love with her. And when he told her he didn't see marriage in his future, he'd meant it. Now, he saw that claim had stemmed from his long-ago wounded pride. He knew now he had never really been in love with Kimberly. Maybe as a teenager he'd been infatuated with her. Reflexively, he'd plugged her face into his dreams, and he had been disappointed because they didn't work out as he'd planned.

Now, he realized he hadn't thought much about her since he'd moved here. Dale had shown him what falling in love was really about.

He glanced up at the house again, noting the rural mailbox on its post was leaning to one side.

Getting out of his car, he crossed the dirt road to the mailbox and straightened it. The pole was so loosely planted in the ground, he knew it would be leaning again after the next gust of wind swept through.

Tomorrow morning, he decided, he would contact a contractor to look at the house. The repairs needed to be done, even if he couldn't complete them himself. No sense in allowing what had once been a fine old house to deteriorate.

He looked again at the dilapidated building. As it appeared in his imagination, patched and polished, it would be a good place for a family to grow together.

His family and Dale's.

But that wasn't what she wanted, he reminded himself.

He had changed his mind. Could she have as well?

Slowly, he walked back to his Corvette, running a hand through his already disheveled hair.

He thought of his sister who had abandoned a promising fashion designing career to marry a forest ranger. Her husband's constant transferring would eliminate any hopes she had of resuming her work. Mace's whole family had questioned how Kit could do that to herself.

Kit had been maddeningly nonchalant about the whole thing. "I had to choose one or the other," she had explained.

He didn't want to force Dale to choose between him or her job. If by some miracle she agreed to marry him, she would be sacrificing a career that meant everything to her. And if she turned him down, she would be responsible for ending their relationship.

And he loved her too much to do it to her.

So, he would fix up this once-charming old house, sell it, and make a nice profit so someone else's family could watch the sun rise over the rolling hills each morning, plant fruit trees in the yard and string lights across the porch at Christmas time.

He would let Dale leave for California believing he was still set against marriage. She would work among the rich and famous, and everything that never happened between them would be his fault.

She wouldn't want to stay anyway, he told himself.

He would have a lifetime without her, and right now he wasn't sure how he could get through the first day.

He took a last glance at the old house. The previous owner, a bachelor who had died in his nineties, had had a reputation for being eccentric. He had left the house to his great nephew. "I'm glad to have the money from selling the place," the nephew had confided to Mace, "But I'd prefer to think Uncle Daniel had enjoyed his life instead of hiding away in there. I'm glad to be rid of it."

No, Mace didn't want to live in that house alone. Funny, being by himself had never bothered him. But then, until now, he had never felt alone.

Early the next morning, Dale stopped at Lila Markum's house on the way to the office to see if the older woman needed anything from town. Mrs. Markum assured her she didn't, but seemed touched that Dale had thought of her.

Because of the detour, Dale arrived at her desk a few minutes later than usual.

As she walked into the office, Jack looked up from his doughnut and carton of chocolate milk. "You're in demand already," he announced. "Someone called you from some town in Illinois. Or maybe it was Michigan."

"What did they want?"

"He didn't seem interested in speaking to anyone but you. A Ted Walker." He handed her a scrap of paper with a number scribbled on it.

Dale inspected the message and sighed. "I hope he's not looking for admission passes. We sold out two weeks ago."

"I thought it might be another job offer."

"Not likely. I haven't given this number out. Besides, I already have a job, remember?"

"This would be closer to home. Why don't you call him? The suspense is killing me."

Dale rolled her eyes. She was going to miss Jack and his constant kidding. Most of the people she knew approached life more seriously. Yet Jack managed to get things done.

Actually, when she returned the call, she discovered the mystery man lived in Ohio, and he wasn't seeking tickets. The pleasant-sounding man had heard about the revival of Meadowside's festival and wanted some pointers in bringing in a crowd for his town's November crafts fair.

"I'd love to help you out, Mr. Walker," she told him. "But I'm caught up in last-minute details for our festival right now. Could you call me back next week?"

She remembered by next week she would be in California.

"Oh, never mind, I won't be here. I'll call you back in a day or two," she promised.

"I don't suppose there's any chance we could persuade you to come and work for us for the next six weeks?" he broached.

"I've already accepted another job."

"I guess you must get assignments pretty far in advance. Everybody, everywhere is holding some kind of event this time of year."

"Oh, I'm just doing this as a favor for my grandfather, filling in some time between jobs."

"You don't know of anyone we might be able to recruit, do you?"

"No, I'm sorry. I don't . . . I'll call you back."

"Please don't wait too long. We're in over our heads here. And we'd appreciate any help you could give us. We're hoping to get people excited about this show."

Dale replaced the receiver thoughtfully. She turned to Jack. "He thought I was a professional festival organizer. I never heard of such a thing."

"Imagine that," Jack quipped absently. "Makes sense. Better planning nets higher profits. In the long run, it would be worth the extra expense. I'm going to recommend the city hire someone next year. Surely we won't be lucky enough to con someone of your capabilities into volunteering two years in a row."

Dale had too much to do to dwell long on Mr. Walker's mistaken assumption.

She began methodically reviewing each of her checklists to ensure she hadn't overlooked a single detail. This was going to be a festival Meadowside would never forget. She knew she wouldn't.

When her eyes tired of reading, she glanced up to spot a shabbily-dressed man on the sidewalk, staring through the plate glass window. His eyes were hidden behind a pair of sunglasses. Just as she looked up, he began moving toward the front door.

Alarmed, Dale stiffened. "That hobo's coming in here," Dale alerted Jack.

Jack looked up, saw the man, and was on his feet before the stranger had shut the door behind him. "Can I help you?" Jack asked authoritatively.

"I doubt it," a cool voice Dale instantly recognized replied. She broke into laughter as Johnny removed the shades, shook his hair free from beneath a baseball cap, and removed the tattered jacket.

"Johnny Reading?" Jack asked incredulously, moving forward to shake the celebrity's hand. "I'm Jack Hall, the chamber of commerce director. I didn't know you'd arrived in town. You should have informed someone . . . I . . . we . . . the local merchants have gifts for you."

Johnny motioned for Jack to come closer.

Jack leaned forward. "Do me a favor, Jack, and send the stuff to a local nursing home and tell the merchants I loved it all, okay? And I'd appreciate it if you'd keep my arrival a secret. I've come here as a favor to Dale, and I don't want to spend my time socializing with the mayor. I came early to spend some time with Dale. This morning, my bodyguard and I have been to the local deli and we'd like Ms. Addison to accompany us on a picnic.''

Dale checked her watch. She couldn't believe it was lunchtime all ready, but the proof was right before her.

''Sounds like fun,'' she agreed, although she'd planned to buy a hamburger at the diner and eat at her desk while she worked through lunch. She felt guilty at how little attention she'd paid to her visiting friend.

Thinking he'd been harsh with Jack, she shot the local man an apologetic look. He was just trying to do his job. Sometimes Johnny tended to overlook all but his own viewpoint. ''Come on along, Jack,'' she invited.

He shook his head. ''Thanks, but I promised my wife I'd have lunch with her at the shop.''

''I wanted you all to myself anyway,'' Johnny said with a wink as he began replacing his disguise.

''I guess we have a lot to catch up on,'' Dale agreed as she grabbed her light jacket off the coat rack. She wouldn't have minded Jack's company at all, but she could understand he wouldn't have felt welcome after the way Johnny had just spoken to him.

Dale already knew Quin, the bodyguard waiting in Johnny's rented car. He was a quiet, sullen man whose presence always made her feel uneasy.

"Hello, Quin," she greeted him as she entered the car.

He gave her a slight nod.

To her chagrin, Quin drove them all the way to the hunting cabin where he and Johnny were staying. "I really don't have a lot of time," she insisted, as they cruised past the city limits.

"You've got to see this place," Johnny insisted. "It's all snug and cozy. The kind of retreat you seem to like these days."

She had to acknowledge the little square log cabin was quaint. Quin spread their lunch on a picnic table to one side of the cabin, then disappeared.

"Unfortunately, the only deli I could find was inside a supermarket," Johnny apologized.

"This is great," Dale assured him, biting into a piece of fried chicken. "Really."

There was far more food than the two of them could ever eat—potato salad, baked beans, coleslaw, rolls, roast beef sandwiches, and cheesecake topped with cherry sauce. Although the air was chilly, sitting outdoors under the bright sunshine was a welcome change from the dark confines of the chamber of commerce office.

Repacking the leftover food, Dale sat back and sipped lemonade from a styrofoam cup. Birds sang overhead, two squirrels raced up a nearby tree, and falling leaves fluttered in the wind.

"Where has Quin gone off to?" she asked. "We should have asked him to eat with us."

"Quin won't starve. Besides, I see him all the time. I get tired of crowds, Dale."

She propped her elbows on the table. "I can understand that. But I do wish you could have been a little more friendly to Jack. He's a nice guy—really funny."

"I can't believe how wrapped up you're getting in all this small-town stuff. I think I've saved you in the nick of time," Johnny replied.

Her eyebrows shot up defensively. "Because I've made friends here?"

"Hey! No offense intended. I can't imagine you staying anywhere without making friends. It's the friend I met last night I'm curious about. He kept giving me the evil eye at your grandparents' house last night, and I don't think it's because he doesn't like my music. What's going on with you two?"

Dale shrugged. "Mace is a good friend," she replied, suddenly uncomfortable. Her feelings about Mace were too personal to share, even with Johnny.

In that moment, she realized she wasn't as certain of his friendship as she'd made herself believe. Maybe Mace's assessment of Johnny's motives wasn't so off-target after all. No, it couldn't be. If Mace was right, everything would change. She wasn't prepared to have her life thrown into turmoil again. Or had it ever really settled down?

"He doesn't look at you like he's seeing his best pal," Johnny observed.

Dale toyed with the edge of a paper sack. She didn't want to discuss Mace with Johnny.

"I'd rather not talk about Mace. At any rate, thank you for getting me out of the office," she told him. "I feel like I should be spending more time with you."

He flashed his movie-star smile. "I can't say I'm not a little disappointed about that. But we'll be seeing more of each other once you get to the coast. It's only a week after all. I'd hate to see anything cause you to back out."

She raised her chin. "I don't intend to."

He moved to the bench on her side of the table, sitting beside her.

Reflexively, Dale tensed, reminding herself Johnny always tended to keep those he cared about physically close. Why did she suddenly feel on edge with him?

"Johnny, you do too much for me. You're responsible for my success with the festival, my getting a new job."

He caught hold of her hand. "Because I enjoy doing anything I can for you, Cowgirl. You know how I feel. Remember that first concert you handled for me? Hardly anyone had heard of me, but you treated me like I was a star, hunting down cheeseburgers at midnight, having that basket of fruit delivered to my hotel room. I'll never forget how absolutely pampered you made me feel. That was the first time I started believing I was going to make it big."

For a reason she couldn't name, Dale resisted his praise. "I'm not sure I do know how you feel," she admitted. "After all, I was just doing what I was supposed to." He had a tight hold on her hand.

His blue eyes skimmed her face, and her intuition told her he was about to try to kiss her. She swallowed hard, not wanting to believe it.

"You're one of the best friends I have, Johnny," she said.

If he'd had anything else on his mind, he changed course. "You're one of the only real friends I have," he replied. "This lifestyle doesn't exactly accommodate the formation of close bonds. You've always been there for me when I needed someone to listen."

Instantly, Dale was ashamed of her suspicions. And she was angry at Mace for having planted those doubts in her mind. A moment ago, she'd nearly been convinced Mace was right. Thankfully, she hadn't said anything that might have hurt Johnny.

She loved Mace, but he didn't know Johnny as she did. Johnny couldn't let just anybody get too close to him. And she'd been on the edge of shutting him out because she'd let Mace brainwash her.

Her overactive imagination was Mace's fault.

"You've boosted my spirits a time or two," she told Johnny. She tossed her empty cup in a trash bag.

"And this has been fun, but I've got to get back to the office."

Johnny gave her one of his winning smiles. "I wish you didn't. I can't believe you're doing all this work for free."

"It means a lot to my grandparents. Besides, it's almost over," she said. And she wondered why the prospect gave her not a sense of relief, but only a feeling of dull resignation.

Chapter Eleven

Mace inhaled deeply before tapping on the front door. Stepping back, he paced the length of the porch, his hands stuffed in his coat pockets.

After what seemed like forever, the door swung open.

Rachel Guthrie, looking cheerful in a dress as golden as the morning, greeted him with a warm smile.

"Mason!" she exclaimed. "This is a surprise. But I'm afraid Dale's not here. She's out at the park. And Sam's gone after a load of pumpkins for her."

"Actually, Mrs. Guthrie, it's you I came to see."

"Me?" she asked, seeming flattered. "How nice.

Well, come on in. I've got coffee and crois-
sants.'' Mace stepped inside. The house was warm,
smelling of coffee, bread, and furniture polish.

Dale's grandmother led him into the dining room.
''Sit down,'' she invited. ''I'll get the coffee. Actually,
it's nice to have company. Can you imagine so much
excitement going on in our little town? With the festival starting tonight, there's been traffic up and down
our quiet little street all morning long. Usually, nobody passes by except the mailman, the garbage col-
lector, and the meter reader. I'll have the coffee in a
jiffy.''

She disappeared into the kitchen.

Mace laughed amiably. ''Dale certainly has drawn
attention to our little town. I saw a CNN truck parked
downtown. Can I help you with something?'' he
asked.

''No. I can handle this,'' she replied. ''You just
sit.''

A few seconds later, she was in the dining room
with a tray.

She set it down, distributing plates and cups.

''There,'' she said, finally sitting down. ''Now, it's
Dale you've come to talk about, isn't it?''

His eyes flew to hers, and he nearly spilled his coffee. ''You don't miss much, do you?'' he asked.

She shook her head. ''Not when it comes to my
granddaughter. In a way I envy her, and in a way I

pity her. Young women today are free to accomplish so much. But they have to give up so many other things my generation enjoyed. Heavens, I wouldn't know what to do if I was faced with so many decisions. Women today don't have time to enjoy the small things, you know. Lifelong friendships through a Tuesday afternoon bridge club, picking out fabric and making curtains just the way you like them, taking time to cook food that tastes good. It's not any wonder she's confused. I wish she felt less driven, but then, she gets that from her father. He was always a go-getter.''

''I'm afraid Dale takes a broader view of life. She's not the bridge club type.''

Rachel's laughter rang like sleigh bells. ''She'd be bored silly doing those things. You can say it. My feelings aren't as fragile as my age might imply.''

Mace left his coffee untouched. ''How do you think she'd feel about fixing up an old house?''

Rachel set her cup down on the saucer. ''Only she can tell you how she feels. I'll tell you one thing though, as much as Dale resists it, she has a sentimental streak.''

''A sentimental streak?''

''It runs in the family. Momentos meant a lot to my mother, as they do to me. Linda, Dale's mother, was a starry-eyed dreamer. Dale gets her flair for organization and management from her dad, but for all she tries to hide it, she's got a romantic notion or two up her sleeve. She thinks she's going to bring back the old times for me and Sam. I love her for it, but when you get to be my age, you realize you can't just summon up times past. Once they're gone, they're gone forever.''

Mace gleaned her meaning. He was on the verge of letting something vital slip away.

''Don't look so distressed,'' she advised. ''Part of life is accepting how precious and unique each moment is.'' She shook her head. ''Unfortunately, you don't discover that until you're old enough to start looking back.''

Mace drummed his fingers on the tabletop. ''This job means so much to Dale. She would never want to stay here,'' he speculated.

''I don't know what's on her mind or in her heart. Sam and I are grateful for the time we've had with her. We missed so much while she was growing up. But if there are choices to be made, I think she should have the chance to make them.''

Mace shook his head. ''I don't think it would be fair to ask her to sacrifice everything she's worked for.''

Rachel's expression grew stern. ''Dale's used to making her decisions and living with them. Nothing's going to make her stay if she doesn't want to. Honestly, Mason. Who are you trying to spare, my granddaughter or yourself? If you love her, as I suspect you do, you'll know what you must do.''

''If I never see another pumpkin in my life, it will be too soon,'' Dale proclaimed as she rearranged the display at the park entrance for the tenth time.

''Let the maintenance people do this,'' Johnny, heavily disguised beside her, suggested.

''No, I've almost got it.'' She shifted a potted yellow mum. ''I want this to be just right.''

Johnny surveyed the decorations. ''Looks fine to me, honey.''

''Maybe we should bring one of the scarecrows out here.''

Johnny clasped a hand to his forehead. ''Dale!''

''I'm sorry. This must be boring for you. Do you want me to drive you back to the cabin?''

''No, thanks. I have Quin around here somewhere. Now, are you going to tell me what's wrong?''

She leveled her glance on her friend.

''You know me too well.''

''So, are you going to reveal what's on your mind?''

Dale set the pumpkin she'd been cradling on a bale of hay. ''I didn't get much sleep last night, thinking about things.''

''This sounds ominous.''

''Johnny, you have been so great to come here and

do this concert. Nobody has ever done anything like this for me.''

His eyes darkened. ''But?''

''I keep asking myself why you're doing all this for me, and I keep telling myself it's because you're my friend.''

''That revelation shouldn't be keeping you awake.''

Her brow creased. ''What would you say if I told you I've been thinking about staying here?''

''I'd say you've gone mad. What are you going to do, clerk in the five-and-ten?''

''We are just friends, aren't we Johnny? I feel like a fool for asking. I know we got all that straightened out long ago, but yesterday I got the funniest feeling maybe one of us was hoping for something else. I have to know the truth before I can go to California.''

Johnny walked over to a bale of hay and sat down. He sighed heavily and removed his dark glasses. ''So, that's it. It's you who knows me too well. You weren't imagining anything yesterday. I'm sorry, Dale, but I can't be your buddy or your big brother. Your the only person in my life that's real to me, and you're too close to my heart for me to keep my distance. I've never gotten over you. Is that really so awful? Think of the team the two of us would make.''

''Oh, Johnny. I can't be what you want.''

''You already are what I want. I don't want to change you.''

"But I don't love you that way. You're too good to settle for that. Someday, you'll find the right person."

"I have."

"No, you haven't."

"It's all right. You don't have to decide today. But I'm warning you once you get to California, I'm not going to give up trying to persuade you to marry me."

"Johnny, I'm not going to California. What you've just told me cinches it."

"I was afraid you were going to say that. Look, just because I made the contacts for this job doesn't mean you have to turn it down. I'm not attaching any strings to the deal."

"I know that. But I can't go. I have a bad feeling about the job. I have all along. I can't explain it. I started on the ground floor with a prospering, growing company once. I don't want to do that same thing all over again. And I don't want to be a continent away from my grandparents. I hope this isn't going to put you in a bad position."

"Don't worry about it. I'm a star. I'm supposed to be a brat, right?"

She smiled slightly, swallowing hard. "If I had known you felt this way, I wouldn't have asked you to do the concert tonight."

"How could you have known when I wasn't being honest with you? Besides, I would have done this for you, regardless."

"You're not making me feel any better."

"I don't want to let you off the hook too easily," he shook his head. "Truthfully, what are you going to do here?"

She shook her hair back. "I have an idea I've been tossing around. It's a risk, but I think I can make it work. You know what? For the first time since the layoff, I don't feel like the world's about to crack in half because of it."

"I can't believe how at home you seem here in Pumpkinville. Or that I won't be seeing you again after tonight."

"Johnny, please don't make me cry. We don't know what will happen."

"But I know you." He placed a hand on her shoulder. "Look, if it's what you really want, I hope things work out with you and Mace."

Her eyes flared. "You know about that too?"

"Dale, you two could barely take your eyes off each other all evening. What do you think prompted me to overplay my hand? I saw I risked losing you either way, most likely to him."

"You know, Johnny, I've been so focused on my career, I guess to a lot of people I came across as selfish. When I first got my job, I was working like a maniac because I had a vision of a good life for myself and my future family. As if I could replace the one I'd lost by working hard. But along the way, I lost my vision. I was working for work's sake. I mean, I didn't know what I was working toward any more. Losing my job was the best thing that could have ever happened to me, or I might have gotten old before I ever realized I was grasping at air. I have a family here, and the rest will work itself out. Even if I have to sell cosmetics.''

''Don't even joke about that. You have a responsibility to use your talents. Remember that. I'm going to miss you, Cowgirl.''

''I'll miss you too, Johnny.''

''Are you sure about this Mace character?''

She nodded, blinking back tears. ''He's strong and good, and I couldn't help falling in love with him. But even if I stay, I don't expect anything to come of it. There's someone else he's never gotten over.''

''If he's as smart as you think he is, I don't think he'll let you get away.''

''Gosh, Johnny. Don't ever believe it's easy for me to give you up.''

She hugged him warmly, and then she did cry.

''Mrs. Markum,'' Mace said as he stopped the older woman. ''Have you seen Dale?''

The park buzzed with activity, the sounds of sawing and hammering echoed across the countryside as booths went up.

The widow turned to him. ''Mr. Travers. Isn't this

wonderful? Meadowside has certainly come to life. We're having such a good time out here. The Happy Needleworkers have one of the best booth spaces, you know. Setting up a booth is so involved, and my daughter's due to arrive in a few hours.''

He had never seen the woman so animated.

''It's good to see you out. Have you seen Dale?''

''I think I saw her about fifteen minutes ago, over by the model train club exhibit.'' She pointed in the direction of the baseball field. ''Did you know she's leaving town tomorrow?''

Not if I can help it, Mace thought.

''You know, as a council member, you should do something to keep the young people here.''

''It's not that simple, but I'll work on it. Thank you,'' he concluded, heading in the direction she'd pointed him.

He spotted Dale leaning over the track. She wore jeans, a New York University sweatshirt, and plaid tennis shoes with her hair pulled back in a ponytail, a clipboard dangling from one hand and a two-way radio fastened to a belt loop.

Watching with fascination as the trains raced around the track, she might have been a teenager instead of the mastermind behind all this.

He had to admit, she'd given this town the boost it had sorely needed.

Sam and his fellow members of the model train club

were arranging miniature buildings and figures around the track.

Sam spotted him and greeted him first. "Good afternoon, Mace."

"Hello, Sam."

Dale's glance swung to meet his.

Her smile radiated like sunshine.

"Hi," she said.

"Hi." He raised the white paper bag he held in his hand. "I brought you some lunch."

"Thanks. I'm starving. Come here, I want to show you something."

Curious, he followed her to the opposite side of the exhibit. In one corner was a miniature carnival, complete with a lighted midway—a revolving carousel and Ferris wheel and moving bumper cars skirted the train track.

"Isn't it precious?" she asked.

He nodded. Her grandmother was right. Like her, in her own way, Dale sought out life's magical little fantasies.

"It reminds me of Meadowside," Dale explained. "The world in miniature."

"I never quite thought of Meadowside that way. How long have you been out here?"

"Since before dawn."

"Let's grab one of the picnic tables. I'd say you're about due for a break."

She headed toward the nearest table.

She settled down on the bench while Mace un-packed submarine sandwiches with dill pickle spears and cans of ice-cold apple juice.

"Your eyes are red," he noted, handing her a paper napkin.

"Allergies," she lied.

He wondered what she had been crying about. Seeing her unhappy riled him. And her refusal to tell him what was wrong disturbed him.

"You weren't arguing with Sam, were you?"

"No. He's been pretty easy-going lately."

"Having you around has made a difference."

"It's the festival that's got him in good spirits."

"You've done a tremendous job here," he said, gesturing toward the activity around them. "I feel guilty that we're not paying you."

"I'm glad I'm not getting paid. I've loved doing this for my grandparents and their neighbors. Seeing it all come together is reward enough. Everyone's pitched in. But I have to admit I'm a little disappointed."

"No one else is. Why?"

"We've had to move Johnny's concert to the largest place in town, the high school football stadium. Thank goodness there wasn't a game tonight. Oh, the festival is going to be a success, but you and Gramps were right. I've turned it into a circus. Tonight's concert will be a far cry from the dance in the little pavilion where Gramps and Grandma met.''

''You can't go back in time,'' he reflected, remembering words he had heard this morning.

''I suppose not.''

''Did your grandfather tell you what the town plans to do with the festival profits?''

''No.''

''We're renovating the old warehouse downtown into a community center. It will be a place to hold meetings, bazaars, performances, after-school programs.''

''It was your idea, wasn't it?''

''One your grandfather immediately backed me on.''

''It's nice to see you both on the same side. In his own grumpy way, he does like you.''

''Dale, do you remember the city council meeting where you got roped into overseeing this festival?''

''Of course.''

''I said then that if anyone could make a success of this festival, I'd hire that person to run my company.''

''If you said any such thing, I don't intend to hold you to it.''

''Yes, I prefer to handle management myself,'' he agreed. ''But I could use you as a sales manager.''

She placed her sandwich on its wrapper. ''You're asking me to stay in Meadowside?''

"Yes."

"And work for you?"

"I don't want you to leave."

Her throat was suddenly too tight for her to swallow. She wanted a future with him, not with his company.

"I can't accept your offer."

His expression darkened.

Dale studied his face. Tenderness and disappointment flooded through her. Staying in Meadowside and knowing she and Mace had no future together was going to be torture for her. She knew the only way she could endure it was to distance herself from him. She didn't tell him she had already decided to stay.

"You don't have to go all the way to California."

"My working for you wouldn't work, and you know it." Leaving her sandwich half-eaten, she checked her watch.

"I've got to meet someone downtown," she excused herself. "Thank you for lunch."

She was gone before Mace could protest.

He could think of no one she could be meeting except Johnny. And that prospect made his chest constrict.

He had blown it, and he hadn't even leveled with her. He just had to accept the fact that nothing on God's earth was going to persuade her to stay in Meadowside. Still, he knew he should have confessed he quite simply wanted to spend the rest of his life loving her.

Twilight cloaked the normally sleepy town of Meadowside. Dale moved silently through the park, making a last check of the booths.

Even though she was satisfied with the lease she'd taken on the small downtown office, her stomach was plagued with butterflies. She had called her first client, Ted Walker and promised to drop a contract in the mail. Come Monday morning, she'd be in business as a special events planning consultant.

The look on Gramp's face when she told him, had confirmed the wisdom of her decision. She was among family here, and it felt good. But except for sharing the news with Rachel, he was sworn to secrecy.

"Mace is bound to notice you're still here sooner or later," he'd grumbled.

She feared Mace would misunderstand why she was staying. But she didn't plan to continue seeing him. She couldn't love half-heartedly. If he truly loved her, he wouldn't hold back because of something that happened in the past. None of that mattered now.

"Good evening," she said to the security guard, one of several who had been hired for this weekend.

"Good evening, Ms. Addison. Shouldn't you be over at the football stadium for the concert?"

She smiled. He didn't look old enough to be out of

high school. "I just wanted to make sure everything here will be ready for tomorrow morning. Do you guys need anything?"

"No. We're all set."

"A pizza and soft drinks are being sent out around eleven."

"Thank you."

Her radio crackled.

She raised it to her ear. Mace's voice greeted her.

Hearing it evoked a poignant sadness within her. What they might've had together could have been wonderful.

"Yes?" she said.

"Dale, you've got to get over here to the stadium. There's a problem with Johnny. He's not here yet."

"Oh, no." Her stomach tightened. She wiped her forehead with her sleeve. "I'll be right there. Sing or something."

"Right. Out."

She replaced the radio. She knew she'd upset Johnny this afternoon, but he would never walk out on her. What if something had happened to him?

She raced to her Grand Am, heading not toward the stadium, but toward the hunting lodge.

Halfway there, she found the rental car parked on the shoulder, Johnny and Quin standing behind the open trunk.

She made an abrupt U-turn.

"Is everything all right?" she called out the window.

"Flat tire," Johnny said with a shrug. "We've got it changed. We're on our way."

"I wish you'd let me send someone to drive you."

He shook his head. "We're off to the airport after the show."

She realized suddenly how all the loose ends of her life were coming together at once. "I wish things could have been different, Johnny."

"Not like I do, Cowgirl."

He looked at her sadly. "Let's go. I intend to put on one dilly of a show tonight."

"I'll see you there."

Mace and her grandparents were waiting for her in the locker room, which had been transformed tonight into a backstage area.

Mace watched her walk in, Johnny and Quin trailing behind her amidst a flock of guards.

Dale came up beside him. Mace leaned close and whispered, "At last. I was beginning to wonder if I would have to get out there and sing."

"They had a flat tire," she explained.

In the midst of all these people, she suddenly felt as though just the two of them were there, like the day they'd walked in the park. Tonight, for the last time, she would remain by his side. She couldn't let go too quickly.

"Let's go watch the concert from the sidelines," she suggested.

"Sure," he agreed.

The crowd roared as Johnny came on stage.

Dale basked in her momentary success. Johnny's songs had never sounded sweeter.

Dale swayed in time with the music, her glance shifting to Mace beside her.

He smiled at her.

Her heart snapped. She smiled back. Reflexively, she took hold of his arm.

Johnny was speaking in the mike. "I want to dedicate this song to a good friend of mine, Dale Addision. If you're having a good time tonight, she's the one responsible."

The opening strains of a ballad broke through thunderous applause.

A sharp elbow nudged Mace's back.

Startled, he turned, only to find Sam staring at him purposefully.

Confused, he returned his attention to the performance.

Once again, Sam nudged him.

This time, Mace caught on.

Couples were beginning to dance along the sidelines and in the aisles. He swept Dale into his arms. She felt so soft and good. He knew he never wanted to let her go.

Pressed against him, Dale closed her eyes. The autumn night filled her senses.

She wanted to stay wrapped in Mace's arms for a long time to come.

Something unexpected settled into her heart. She opened her eyes, looked into the clear sky and the shining stars overhead.

Her eyes drifted to her dance partner. Would he think she was star-struck if she tried to explain that in that instant she felt, no she knew, her mother would have approved of this match. It was as if her mother, the woman she couldn't remember, were watching now.

She rested her head against Mace's chest. His hand brushed her silky hair, and he knew he couldn't let her go so easily. He couldn't let her go at all.

He stopped dancing.

"Marry me!" he requested.

Dale gestured to indicate she couldn't hear him over the music.

"Marry me!" he repeated.

Again, she gestured apologetically.

Just as he shouted his proposal a third time, the song came to a sudden end. His words echoed through the stadium.

After a long silence, the audience broke into cheers.

And since Dale knew he'd never hear her over the noise, she replied by leaning up to kiss him.

And the power of the kiss conveyed that he understood.

Her heart skyrocketed. Funny, she'd found love where and when she'd least expected it. But maybe it was meant to be all along. Maybe her involvement in this festival had been more than just a sentimental notion after all.

Later, she would tell Mace about the plans for her new business.

But she had many more important things to tell him first.